Reunion
ISLAND
MURDER IN PARADISE SERIES

Reunion
ISLAND

RACHEL WOODS & ANGEL VANE

BONZAIMOON BOOKS

BONZAI
MOON

BonzaiMoon Books LLC
Houston, Texas
www.bonzaimoonbooks.com

Editing by Kelly Hartigan of Xterra Web
http://editing.xterraweb.com

Book cover designed by Deranged Doctor Design
http://www.derangeddoctordesign.com

ISBN 978-1-943685-07-3 (Print)

Thank you God for giving me creative ideas and the ability to write. Thank you to my family --- my extraordinary sister and my favorite mother! A special thanks to the Chocolate Divas and the wonderful trip we took to Punta Cana which provided the inspiration for this book!
~Rachel Woods

Thanks to God for calling those things which be not as though they were. Thanks to my mother, who inspires me daily by instilling a perpetual sense that there is nothing I can't do and to my sister, who finds endless ways to push me outside of my comfort zone.
~Angel Vane

Thank you to Marija Lulkoska for naming the male lead in the book.
~Rachel & Angel

Prologue

I'm going to die tonight, he thought, gazing at the amber liquid his favorite bartender, Ratcliff, expertly poured into his glass.

"You doing all right tonight, Mr. Jameson?" Ratcliff asked, screwing the cap back on the bottle of whiskey he preferred, the only drink he ever ordered when he patronized the Purple Gecko. A local bar on Sandy Coral Road, it was in a neighborhood called Handweg Gardens, considered the wrong side of the island, an area where tourists were warned not to wander around alone at night. He liked the Purple Gecko because it wasn't busy during the week. On the weekend it was a madhouse of adventurous tourists and locals, deafening reggae, thick clouds of weed-laced smoke, and raucous behavior.

"I'm okay, Ratcliff," he said, even though he wasn't.

He had stopped being okay ten minutes ago, when the door opened and he'd turned, wondering who might be about to enter the seedy dive.

"You need anything else, Mr. Jameson, you let me know," Ratcliff said and then returned to his spot behind the bar, where he began polishing glasses as he stared at a cricket match on the small black-and-white television mounted on the wall.

"Sure thing," the man said, clutching the shot glass with trembling fingers as he brought it to his mouth and took another sip.

He'd nearly gagged when she'd walked in, tall and lithe, nothing but dangerous curves beneath a clingy red strapless dress. A mane of luxurious raven hair tumbled down her back as she navigated the maze of tables, heading to the bar. He could scarcely believe it was her. Amal Shahin. For a moment, he'd thought the whiskey was giving him some sort of alcoholic hallucination, but no, it was Amal. He'd never forget the fierce, intimidating beauty.

He let out a long, shaky exhale, staring as she stood at the bar ordering a drink. Amal would kill him tonight. Pressing the barrel against his forehead, she would squeeze the trigger.

Amal Shahin didn't look like a cold-blooded killer.

She looked like what she was perfect for—a fast and dirty fuck in the back of his car followed by a hasty departure with no need for awkward goodbyes. Hadn't their first time together been quick and nasty? Tumultuous and explosive. Separation without explanation. No need for discussion when there were no ridiculous expectations like love or commitment, no need to let feelings get in the way of a good thing. And it had been damn good. Sexy and experimental, the best kind of decadent debauchery. Almost too much of a good thing.

Now, it was a good thing about to go very bad.

He took a drink but the whiskey which had soothed him moments ago felt like acid going down his throat and soured in his stomach.

His mind raced. He struggled to control his thoughts, to prioritize his current predicament. He needed to figure out his next move, but her presence, so alluring and tempting, had shocked him, and options eluded him. He didn't have a plan, didn't know what to do other than hope he could get away before she put a bullet between his eyes. Picking up the wine she'd requested, Amal turned and smiled at him, raising the glass.

Hopes fading, he downed the remaining whiskey, now more convinced than ever that this would be his last night alive.

Chapter One

It was a magical day, thought Vivian Thomas, smiling as she inhaled the salty ocean breeze and gazed toward the miles of pristine pink powdery sand and clear turquoise waters of the Caribbean Sea.

Earlier in the week, there had been predictions of rain in St. Killian, one of the islands in the Palmchat Island chain, but the weather forecast had been wrong. Bright and sunny with brilliant white popcorn clouds, it was the kind of day the Palmchat Island Tourist Board would proclaim was perfect for a "money shot"—a photograph used on the island's official website, designed specifically to entice and mesmerize.

Even more than the wonderful weather, the day was perfect because Vivian was in the company of one of her best friends in all the world, Amal Shahin, her closest confidant for the past ten years. They'd met in high school and had immediately bonded.

Seated around a table at Dizzy Jenny's, the ritzy yet casual beachside restaurant popular with the yachting crowd and local dignitaries, they enjoyed appetizers as they rehashed old tales from their days in high school.

Amal had arrived on the island around nine this morning. Vivian had waved and jumped up and down as her friend hurried across the tarmac to the open-air terminal where she was waiting. Hugs and tears and laughs ensued. College and careers had separated them for stretches of time, but they made an effort to call each other at least once a week. Still, there was nothing like seeing her best friend in person.

Two weeks ago, during one of their weekly chats, Amal announced her intentions to visit the island—a trip that was long overdue. Amal had been trying to fulfill the promise she'd made to visit Vivian, but most, if not all, of her time was dedicated to Phoenix—the medical spa she'd opened two years ago. She'd been too busy to carve out time for a vacation.

A year and a half had flown by since they'd last seen each other, but Vivian clearly remembered the cold, snowy day in March. Hiding out at her mother's winter home in Aspen, Vivian had been in the throes of self-imposed exile when Amal had shown up at the door, determined to convince Vivian not to give up on life. Vivian's world had been shattered by disappointment and devastation, but Amal's blunt, no-bullshit, tough love had been encouraging and empowering, rousing Vivian from the depths of misery.

After Vivian had instructed an airport employee to load Amal's luggage in the back of her Range Rover, she herded her friend into the SUV. Anxious to share her island home, Vivian had taken the long, winding route, pointing out landmarks and scenic spots. Several times, she stopped the Range Rover and hustled Amal out of the car for photo ops in front of gorgeous seascapes. Four hours later, they arrived at Vivian's spacious condo, where Amal would spend the next seven days.

"So, I know you don't pimp the island for the Palmchat tourist office anymore," Amal began, grabbing a goat fritter. "But, I read the guide you wrote—which was excellent, not surprisingly—and I didn't see anything about where to get some good D on this island."

Shaking her head at Amal's amusingly crude comment, Vivian followed her friend's gaze to the bar, where several young St. Killian wait staff clustered, laughing and talking with a trio of bartenders. It wasn't the first time Amal had glanced toward the bar. Vivian wondered if Amal had set her sights on one of the waiters? Maybe the tall guy? Or perhaps the guy with the athletic frame and lean muscles?

Vivian had no doubt Amal would find someone suitable for her tropical fantasies. Raven-haired, tawny-hued Amal was smoking hot and never had a problem getting men to fall in love with her.

Moments later, the waiter brought their drinks. Vivian had suggested palmitos, the local St. Killian favorite, featuring mulled pineapples, rum, and mint, but Amal had requested a glass of pinot noir.

"Okay, Amal, now that we have libations, you know what time it is," Vivian announced, barely able to contain her excitement. "Let's play raise a glass!"

The raise a glass game, which she and Amal had created following high school graduation during the summer before they'd separated to attend their respective colleges, was similar to a toast. Raising a glass was their special acknowledgment of past events, present circumstances, or future hopes and dreams.

"So, I'll raise a glass to the present because I'm so happy and excited to be right here, right now, with my best friend that I love and adore!" said Vivian. "You're like the sister I never wanted!"

Amal rolled her eyes, smiling, and then glanced at her phone, face up on the table near her appetizer plate. "Funny."

"Seriously, Amal," Vivian said. "I'm so glad you're here."

Amal tilted her head, her expression probing, circumspect.

Wary, Vivian asked, "What is it?"

"Nothing," Amal said, voice rising an octave in mock innocence. "Just ... I have a confession."

"A confession?"

"Remember how I told you I was too busy with Phoenix to

visit?" Amal asked as she picked up the buzzing cell phone and frowned. "Well, I lied."

"You lied?" Vivian asked, curious as she saw the crease between Amal's brows deepen. "Why?"

Amal gave her a sly smile, but it seemed a bit forced, Vivian noted. Amal swiped a thumb across the cell phone, lips pursed in disgust, and then she smiled again, a bit brighter.

"I wasn't too busy to come," Amal confessed. "I was just hoping you would come to your senses and leave St. Killian, and then I wouldn't have to come here to visit you, but you're still hiding out in paradise so…"

"Amal, please, don't go there." Vivian shook her head and took another sip of her drink, her wariness turning to discomfort. "We've already had the 'Vivian shouldn't have moved to St. Killian' conversation before, too many times."

"Obviously, we haven't had the conversation enough because you're still hiding out in paradise," Amal said. "I still can't believe you moved here."

"You say 'here' like I'm living in some overcrowded third-world slum," Vivian said. She knew the reason for Amal's disbelief, which had everything to do with Vivian's decision to make a permanent move to the island at the conclusion of a one-month temporary assignment for the department of tourism.

At a party hosted by the tourism minister, the editor of the *Palmchat Gazette* had approached her with a potential job offer, and Vivian jumped at the chance to work for the award-winning publication.

Amal had been less than thrilled when Vivian accepted the *Palmchat Gazette* job. She'd accused Vivian of hiding out on an island because she was too afraid to face the disappointment which had been the reason behind her rash decision to abandon her job at *The Washington Post*.

Countless times, Vivian had tried to explain why she'd chosen to live in paradise. She was grateful for the lazy, laid-back, "island time" pace. St. Killian was different from life in Africa, but she'd needed the change and wanted a new life.

Following the personal setbacks she'd endured, Vivian had been desperate to turn her back on her former life and all the memories associated with the woman she'd once been—a woman hopelessly in love with a man she'd foolishly thought she'd be with forever.

Leo Bronson. The man who had captured her heart the moment they'd met and then crushed it five years later.

"Look around, Amal," Vivian advised, snatching another fritter from the platter. "There's nothing but blue skies, palm trees, and white sand beaches for as far as the eye can see. This is paradise. Why wouldn't I want to live here?"

"I don't have an issue with you living in paradise," Amal conceded, though Vivian suspected she was about to make a point, one Vivian wouldn't be able to dispute. "I have an issue with why you want to live here. You and I both know that you didn't pack your bags and head to the tropics for the palm trees and white sand beaches. You stayed in paradise because—"

"We both know why I stayed in St. Killian." Vivian grabbed a goat fritter and tore into it, chewing angrily. "I was offered a job with the *Palmchat Gazette,* and—"

"You will never convince me that you're fulfilled and satisfied writing puff pieces for some island rag—a job you are horribly overqualified for."

Vivian exhaled. "I took the job at the *Palmchat Gazette* because it was a good opportunity."

"You didn't get a degree in journalism from Columbia University just to end up writing about the top ten things to do in St. Killian."

"The *Palmchat Gazette* is an award-winning publication, I'll have you know," Vivian said. "I write all kinds of stories about crime and corruption. And, no, St. Killian is not the Sudan, but I do enjoy the work I'm doing. Besides, aren't you glad I'm not in Africa anymore? Remember how upset you were when I told you I was working on that piece about the Ugandan warlord's son? Chasing deranged dictators is dangerous."

"Vivian, you're an amazing badass investigative journalist," said Amal. "You should not be wasting your skills, writing about stolen surfboards and hotel crime."

"Why is it so hard for you to believe that I like my job, and my life, in St. Killian?" Vivian asked.

"I don't believe it because it's not true," Amal said. "You decided to stay in St. Killian to avoid dealing with what happened between you and Leo."

"I know that's what you think." Vivian bristled, annoyed by her best friend's assessment. "But, that's not true."

"Deny it all you want," Amal said. "We both know why you don't want to go back to Africa, and it's not because you're afraid of some crazy dictator. You're afraid to see Leo."

Shaking her head, Vivian wanted to tell Amal she was wrong, but the words wouldn't come.

"If you go back to Africa, you know you'll cross paths with Leo, the love of your life," Amal said. "I know your feelings for him haven't changed. You still love him. You still want to be with him. That's why you're terrified of seeing him again. I understand that."

"How could you possibly understand, Amal? You've never been in love," Vivian reminded her. "You've never wanted to fall in love, never wanted to be in a committed relationship. You just go from guy to guy to guy."

"Yeah, and that works for me, for now anyway," Amal said, her tone a tad softer. "But who knows, in the future, maybe if I found the right guy, I just might give him my heart."

Vivian snorted. "I'll believe that when I see it."

Amal shrugged and gave her a smug smile. "Well, you might see it very soon, so get ready to start believing."

"Are you trying to tell me something?" Vivian asked, curious and excited. "Are you seeing someone?"

"I might be," said Amal, her tone vague.

"Wait, you might be seeing someone, and you haven't told me?" Vivian stared at Amal.

"Don't try to get me in a white dress. It's not serious—yet." Amal laughed.

"Well, anyway, enough about me," said Vivian, lifting her palmito from the table. "Your turn to raise a glass."

"Give me a minute," Amal requested, grabbing a goat fritter from the platter between them. "I need to think."

"You need to think?" Vivian shook her head and laughed. "Amal, you have so many things to raise a glass to! For one, your dream business endeavor, Phoenix, the premier medical spa catering to A-list celebrities, billionaire socialites, debutantes, and fashionistas all over the world."

"Not exactly, not just yet, but soon," Amal said. "My clientele is still mostly bored rich housewives whose faces might shatter into a million pieces if they get another Botox injection, but I can't complain. Their seething, unrepentant vanity pays the bills. For the most part, anyway."

"For the most part?" Vivian questioned, taking another sip of her palmito.

"Well, you know …" Amal exhaled under her breath as her cell phone buzzed again.

"Everything okay?" Vivian asked as Amal snatched the phone from the table and frowned once more, staring at the screen.

Her thumbs stabbing the small QWERTY keyboard, Amal said, "Businesses take time to get established, to make a profit."

"Are you having problems?" Vivian asked, concerned.

"What?" Amal stared at her, a trace of suspicion in her dark eyes. "No, I mean, it's just that being your own boss is hard work."

Amal's phone buzzed.

Vivian asked, "You sure everything is okay?"

"Yeah, well, sort of," Amal said, distracted by the phone. "I'm dealing with a new vendor and a new administrative assistant—Snowdrop Sanders. Can you believe that's her real name? Anyway, can I tell her to call me at your house in a few hours? That okay?"

Vivian nodded and gave Amal the number to her condo, which Amal texted to her assistant.

After dropping the phone into her purse, Amal said, "Okay, that's taken care of, so there should be no more interruptions."

"Good," Vivian said. "And your sixty seconds are up, so what are you raising a glass to?"

"I want to raise a glass to myself," Amal said. "Because no one is ever going to make a fool of me again."

"What do you mean by that?" Vivian questioned, staring at her best friend. "Who made a fool of you?"

Hesitating, Amal took a drink of her wine and then cursed.

"What is it?" Vivian asked.

"Well, it's not pinot noir, which is what I asked for," Amal fumed, beckoning for a waiter. "It's pinot grigio."

The waiter arrived with an expansive smile. "How may I help you, beautiful ladies?"

Amal glared at him. "Were you paying attention when I gave you my drink order?"

His smile wavered. "Yes, ma'am—"

"You couldn't have been paying attention," Amal said. "Otherwise, you would have heard me request pinot noir."

"Yes, ma'am, I remember." He nodded. "You ordered the pinot noir."

"Then why did you bring me pinot grigio?"

Bristling from the rebuke, the waiter said, "I'm sorry, ma'am, I—"

"I don't need your apologies," Amal snapped. "Just bring me my pinot noir. Now. Please."

With a slight bow of deference, the waiter scurried off to do Amal's bidding.

"Seriously, Amal?" Vivian asked. "Did you have to bite his head off?"

"He needs to do his job," Amal said, unwilling to cut the waiter any slack. "And, I need to go to the ladies room. I'll be right back."

Chapter Two

In the ladies room, Amal closed and locked the stall door and then leaned against it. Removing her cell phone from her purse, she accessed the last text message she'd received. Reading it, she wondered how the hell she could have been so stupid. How could she have allowed herself to be scammed, duped?

Two years ago, she became the owner of Phoenix, a medical spa which offered age-defying medical treatments and state-of-the-art products and services with guaranteed results. She envisioned Phoenix as a leader in the aesthetic industry, dedicated to providing the best in personal enhancement. By her estimation, Amal figured her success would be effortless, inevitable, and destined.

During her final year in graduate school, for one of her classes, the final exam required students to create a business plan outlining a vision for reviving a failing business. Amal had chosen the low-rent medical spa where she worked part-time as a receptionist. The assignment had been a piece of cake for Amal. The spa was rarely booked, and she often passed the time making lists of reasons why the spa wasn't successful and outlining the changes she would implement to make it a premier exclusive establishment.

Four months later, when she graduated, she turned down several lucrative job offers and decided instead to bring her business plan assignment to fruition. The only good thing about the medical spa was its location, in the heart of Palm Beach, a ritzy town with looks-obsessed women who had access to disposable income.

Amal persuaded banks to loan her the capital needed to make the owner an offer he wasn't about to refuse. A few angel investors helped fund the massive renovations to the building's exterior and interior.

A year later, she changed the name of the facility to Phoenix, which symbolized the origins of the business, from disaster to triumph. Phoenix would be a medical spa where women and men could overcome whatever physical destruction had befallen them and ascend to a beautiful victory.

More importantly, Phoenix would boast amazing revenues and avenues for growth.

Reality had come quickly, swiftly. Most new businesses failed within the first year. Those that didn't fail rarely made a profit for the first three to five years. Amal hadn't been in the mood to wait five years before her bank accounts were in the black, so she'd expanded the services the spa provided.

Soon, she began to amass the amounts of money she deserved to make.

Things had been going well until six months ago. One ill-fated decision and now everything she'd worked for was at risk. Her entire world might come crashing down around her, but Amal would be damned if she was crushed.

Despite her frustration and anger, Amal had a plan. She was nothing if not cunning and creative, and her idea was high risk, but she had no choice. She had been burned, charred, and scarred because she had played with the wrong kind of fire.

She planned to rise from the ashes.

Her cell phone buzzed again.

Yanking the phone from her purse, Amal glared at the display. Another text, one she'd been waiting for. Amal accessed the message and read it: *I got what you need*

Relief snaking through her, Amal responded. *9 mm?*

A few seconds later, the phone buzzed again. *Yeah meet me at the bar*

Taking a deep breath, Amal summoned courage, reminding herself of the reason for the trip to St. Killian. Paradise wasn't really about rest, relaxation, and reunion. Her true motive was revenge, retribution, and retaliation. She would be vindicated. And if someone had to die so she could get back what had been viciously stolen from her, then so be it.

Chapter Three

As lively calypso music mixed with the soft din of casual conversation around her, Vivian reflected on Amal's opinions of her career choices, trying to be objective and not feel defensive.

Vivian, you're an amazing badass investigative journalist. You should not be wasting your skills.

Despite what Amal thought, Vivian didn't consider her work at the *Palmchat Gazette* a waste of her talent. She enjoyed the job and had plenty of opportunities to write complex stories with multiple angles. When she'd first taken the job, Vivian had been grateful for the distraction of a different landscape, but now she was no longer interested in covering wars in Africa, risking life and limb in lawless lands. The Sudan had taken a toll on her spirit and her soul. And yet, her heart had suffered the worst, because of Leo.

The truth was, she hadn't been chased out of Africa by a tribal dictator, as some of her former colleagues believed. She'd fled because of her stupidity and foolishness because she'd been misguided enough to believe in happily ever after.

Her fairy tale had turned into a nightmare, and reality had been devastating, confusing, and frustrating. The reality was that Leo didn't want to get married. When he'd first told her, Vivian hadn't wanted to believe him. For some reason, she'd been dumb enough to believe she could change his mind. After all, his feelings for her hadn't changed. By his admission, Leo had claimed to love her still. Somehow, someway, Vivian thought she could convince Leo to walk down the aisle and into together forever as long as they both lived. She was no longer living with those delusions.

Vivian ate the last goat fritter and then started on the jerk fries. Amal had been right. Vivian did still love Leo. Still, she'd spent the last year trying to get over him, trying to get past the disappointment. She wasn't completely healed, but her wounds were no longer raw and gaping. She didn't want Leo to walk back into her life and derail what little progress she'd made.

Leo's rejection of her hopes and dreams had left Vivian feeling inadequate, unworthy, and ashamed. She'd been disconsolate and, more than anything, confused. Leo claimed to love her, claimed she was the only woman he'd ever loved and the only woman he wanted to love, and yet when he should have made her dreams come true, he had destroyed them with five words.

Words she now hated.

As a woman who was passionate about words, relying on them for her livelihood and enjoyment, Vivian never thought she would hate any words. And yet, on that hot Sunday morning in Juba, the Sudanese metropolis where they were based, at the Royal Palace Hotel, less than a mile from the White Nile River, those five horrible words uttered by Leo had nearly destroyed her.

Popping a fry into her mouth, Vivian watched as Amal sauntered alongside the U-shaped bar, turning more than a few heads.

Instead of heading back to their table, Amal sat on an empty stool near the end of the bar.

What was Amal up to, Vivian wondered. The bartender approached Amal, but she waved him away. Moments later, a waiter walked up to Amal. Tall and good-looking, he had lean muscles and short, blond-tipped dreadlocks. As he lowered his head to whisper in Amal's ear, Vivian frowned. She recognized the waiter. The focus of an investigative crime story at the *Palmchat Gazette*, the waiter was rumored to be involved with a gang of criminals who got jobs at high-end restaurants with the intent of stealing from drunk, distracted tourists. Thinking about the story, Vivian remembered there hadn't been enough solid evidence against the waiter to bring any charges against him.

Detective Baxter François, the lead detective with the St. Killian police department, had told Vivian the waiter was savvy. She and the detective had developed a polite, if not friendly, relationship. François had admitted that the waiter was most likely guilty but sly enough to make sure there were no connections between him and the crime.

After the waiter had walked away, quickly disappearing into the shadowy interior of the restaurant, Amal made her way back to the table.

"The stupid waiter still hasn't brought my pinot noir?" Amal asked, taking her seat again.

"I'm sure it's on the way," Vivian reassured her, somewhat troubled by Amal's conversation with the shady waiter.

Shaking her head, Amal said, "Who do you have to blow to get a glass of wine in this joint?"

"What were you and that waiter talking about?" Vivian questioned.

"I knew you were watching me," Amal said, her smile naughty. "His name is Landon, and I gave him my number. He claims to have a foot-long, but I told him 'Honey, twelve inches isn't going to cut it. I need a two-by-four'!"

Vivian cackled at her best friend's unabashed bawdiness, but Amal's encounter with the waiter still bothered her.

Chapter Four

Lounging on a chaise on the terrace, Vivian stared at the Caribbean Sea, thinking about Amal's toast.

I want to raise a glass to myself because no one is ever going to make a fool of me again. What could the toast mean? Had someone tried to fool her? Was her best friend having some personal problems? Maybe, but if so, Vivian knew Amal would turn things around. Her best friend had always been able to pull off a surprise victory. She was smart and determined, able to go from tragedy to triumph.

Amal would always rise from the ashes.

Thinking about Amal made Vivian wonder where she was. Rising from the chaise, Vivian crossed the terrace. Walking through the opened pocket doors, Vivian headed into the den, thinking about Amal's conversation with the waiter. When they'd returned to the condo, Amal had retired to her room to freshen up, while Vivian had taken a moment to search the newspaper's database of articles, looking for more information about the waiter.

After finding the story, Vivian reread it a few times. The waiter's name was Landon George, and just as she remembered, he hadn't been charged with a crime. Still, Vivian didn't trust him.

When she'd interviewed him, Landon had been dismissive and smug, as though daring her to prove his guilt.

Heading down the hall, Vivian noticed the door to Amal's bedroom was ajar. Her best friend's voice exploded from the room.

"I'm going to kill him!" Amal swore. "Son of a bitch!"

In the ten years she'd known Amal, Vivian had never heard her best friend sound so infuriated, so full of rage. Amal had never backed down from a confrontation. Her best friend had always been the kickass take-no-prisoners type who didn't take crap from anyone and had always stood up for herself.

She wasn't one to start a fight but always finished it.

Vivian had witnessed Amal's anger before, many times, but the wrath permeating Amal's voice, fueling her words, made Vivian think of a crazed Liberian general she'd interviewed. He'd spewed deranged ideology. His hatred was almost like desire, a passionate longing to kill his enemies. Shaken, disturbed by her comparison of Amal to an insane tribal leader, Vivian walked to the door and knocked. "Amal?"

"One second," Amal called out and then lowered her voice to a whisper of tense words Vivian couldn't understand.

A moment later, Amal opened the door wide and beckoned for Vivian to come in.

"Everything okay?" Vivian ventured, stepping over the threshold.

"Everything is great, especially this room." Amal twirled around a few times, arms outstretched, like Wonder Woman, and then plopped down on the edge of the bed, laughing. "And this condo. Beyond gorgeous!"

"I'm pretty happy with it," Vivian said, sitting in the chair across from the bed.

Her unit, on the southwestern section of the sprawling grounds, featured walls of French windows and doors, offering dazzling views of the Caribbean Sea both at sunrise and sunset. A two-story model, the lower level was comprised of a cavernous living room, spacious kitchen and dining room, and an opulent master suite. Through the kitchen, there was an attached garage, and from the garage, a door opened to a quaint, picturesque courtyard.

Upstairs was a large den, a study, and three guest bedrooms. Collapsible pocket doors in the den opened to the second-floor terrace, perfect for relaxing and entertaining.

"Let me guess," Amal said. "Mom and Dad helped, right?"

"A little," Vivian admitted, nodding.

"Yeah, right," Amal said, laughing as she threw an accent pillow in Vivian's direction. "From the looks of this place, I'll bet they helped out more than just a little."

"Oh, shut up," Vivian warned and launched the accent pillow toward Amal, who ducked to avoid being hit.

"By the way," Amal said. "I read your article about St. Mateo on the plane. Very interesting and informative. Made me want to go there."

"Actually, the article could have been way more exciting if I had been allowed to investigate a rumor I overheard, but ..."

"What rumor?" Amal asked.

"Apparently, there is a secret exclusive sex hotel on St. Mateo called the Heliconia."

"Are you serious?" Amal cackled mischievously, clapping her hands. "Maybe I should have gone to St. Mateo."

"It's just a rumor," Vivian said, laughing. "Probably not true."

"That sucks." Amal stood and walked to the full-length mirror in the corner near the wardrobe.

Clearing her throat, Vivian said, "So, I hope I didn't interrupt your phone call."

"You didn't," Amal said, scrutinizing her reflection, scowling slightly.

Vivian hesitated and then said, "The conversation sounded intense."

Amal faced her, eyes hard and shrewd. "You were listening?"

"Well, no, not really," Vivian stammered, taken aback by Amal's intense glare.

"What did you hear?" Amal demanded, a fierceness in her gaze Vivian didn't recognize or understand.

"I heard you say that you were going to kill someone."

Amal glared, and Vivian saw a quick flash of hatred in her friend's dark eyes, but then Amal glanced away for a moment, and when she looked at Vivian again, the ire was gone, replaced by frustration.

"I'm sorry." Amal exhaled, shaking her head. "I didn't mean to snap at you. I'm just ..."

"Just what?"

Amal shook her head. "That was Snowdrop, my new assistant I told you about."

"Is her name really Snowdrop?" Vivian asked, skeptical.

Chuckling, Amal said, "That is literally her name. Beyond ridiculous. Anyway, she is a long-term temp, and she has no critical thinking skills. But she can type one hundred and fifteen words per minute, and she's a master at Word and Excel. She's like an administrative savant."

Vivian laughed.

"Anyway, there's an issue with a new vendor," Amal said. "He's who I was threatening to kill. He claims there's a problem with my purchase order for the new massage tables I requested which I need, like, yesterday. He's refusing to deliver the tables. I really need to stay on top of the situation. That's why I asked you if Snowdrop could call me here at the condo."

"Oh, that's right," Vivian said, not sure she believed Amal's story, not sure a massage table vendor could invoke the seething rage she'd heard in Amal's tone. She didn't want to prod and pry, didn't want to treat her best friend to a St. Killian Inquisition. Besides, what did she know about the medical spa business? An unreliable vendor could very well inspire murderous anger.

Amal said, "Once I get this issue with the vendor under control,

I'll be completely free to relax and enjoy these next seven days in paradise."

"Well, I hope the issue with the vendor won't stop you from going to the street circus tonight."

"The street circus?"

"It's so much fun," Vivian promised. "The street circus is like a huge block party with a carnival vibe."

"Sounds like fun, but …"

"But … what?" Vivian asked. "Don't tell me you don't want to go. Amal, you have to go."

"No, I really want to go, and I plan to go," Amal said. "But I also made some other plans, too."

"What other plans?" Vivian stared at Amal, slightly suspicious.

"Other plans with Landon, the hot-to-death waiter from Dizzy Jenny's," Amal said. "Hopefully, anyway. He may, or may not, call me, but if he does, I want to be available."

"Yeah, about that …" Vivian said.

"About what?" Amal asked.

"Hooking up with Landon."

"I know I shouldn't," Amal said, giggling. "But, I can't help myself. And, believe it or not, but it's been beyond forever since I got laid."

Vivian nodded, noncommittal, saying nothing. She did know, actually, what it was like to go through a sex drought. She'd been celibate since—

Stopping the thought, Vivian refused to go there, afraid of getting caught up in the memories.

Focusing on Amal, she said, "I know some things about Landon."

Affecting a comical, horror-stricken look, Amal said, "Don't tell me. He lied about the foot-long."

After a sigh, Vivian told Amal about Landon's brush with the law and possible criminal ties.

"But, he wasn't charged with anything, right?" Amal asked, glancing away.

"No, he wasn't," Vivian said. "But—"

"Then it doesn't matter," Amal said, crossing her left leg over the right. "He's not a crook, so he's okay in my book."

Shaking her head, Vivian said, "Just be careful if you decide to hook up with Landon, okay?"

With a sly grin and a sassy wink, Amal pointed to a red strapless sundress hanging on the bathroom door and asked, "What do you think about that dress for the street circus?"

"That's hot," Vivian said, approving. "And you know what? I have the perfect red scarf to go with that sizzling red dress."

"Will the scarf help me get lucky?" Amal asked.

"Maybe," Vivian said, heading out of the room. "But hopefully not with Landon."

Chapter Five

"How long does it take to fall out of love?" Vivian cocked her head to the side and peered into the eye of the seagull perched on the edge of the railing. Staring at the torn-up pieces of bread in her hand, the seagull gave no response. Not that Vivian expected one. This wasn't a Disney movie after all. This was her fucked-up life.

"No answer? Some substitute for a best friend you are." Vivian hunched her shoulders and leaned slightly to throw the bread over the railing. The seagull plummeted to the concrete below, landing softly, and began to feast.

Vivian gazed at the horizon. The sizzling sunshine and postcard view from her condo balcony weren't enough to counter the storm brewing inside of her. She needed her best friend right now. Where the hell was Amal? She glanced at her watch; it was a quarter after eleven in the morning. How long did it take to bang a sexy waiter into oblivion?

Punching her fists into her thighs, Vivian let out a low moan.

How could she have let this happen?

Last night, in one foolish moment of weakness, she'd unraveled over a year's worth of progress in finding herself and reconnecting with the woman she'd been. Her new life, rebuilt and renewed from the devastation of her past, had begun to crumble. This beautiful island that had healed her soul and spirit, the place she'd grown to love, would never be the same for her now.

The largest of the Palmchat Islands, St. Killian was flat and sprawling with endless miles of pink sand beaches bordering the neighborhoods and jungles. The government had quickly learned to prostitute the allure of the island, monetizing its natural attributes to become a mecca for commerce. Developers had flocked there, building easily on the terrain, leaving behind a pristine mirage of resorts circling almost the entire coastline. With the resorts came tourists and a thriving economy, supporting a healthy base of well-to-do St. Killian locals and ex-pats.

Vivian had been lured to the island initially for a short-term assignment to write the groundbreaking, first-ever Palmchat Island Tourist Guide commissioned by the local government. Traveling and researching the islands in the chain had started the process of healing Vivian's soul. On her journeys through the islands, she encountered, time and again, evidence of survival in the local people, customs, and environment. More than surviving, the people and the land thrived from adversity and emerged better from tragedy. Nothing could dampen the spirit of the islands, not the hurricanes, water pollution, oil drilling, drug trafficking, or mafia infiltration. With each struggle, the island chain and its people were made more glorious. Witnessing this time and again had been an inspiration to Vivian.

Working on the tourist guide had also opened her eyes to a thriving community of writers, with several Caribbean-themed magazines and an award-winning newspaper all headquartered in St. Killian. Her passion for writing and investigating had been reignited, and she'd made another hasty decision, but this time she knew in her heart this one was for all the right reasons. Accepting a staff writer position, she'd packed up everything she owned and relocated to the island permanently, ignoring her mother's protests and the wariness in her father's eyes.

Submerging herself in each article on crime and corruption in the Caribbean had been the cleansing needed to turn her life around and reconnect with the woman she'd lost. Her stories were groundbreaking and riveting, giving her renewed confidence and a quick promotion to senior staff writer. The life she'd obliterated was being renewed, bridges burned were repaired, and the broken heart that had started her freefall had begun to mend.

The painful, bittersweet memories of her life in Africa were no longer sharp and debilitating, fading to a muted and transient presence that no longer haunted each of her days. That was, until three months into working for the paper, it was purchased by Burt Bronson.

Burt Bronson was legendary in the publishing industry, a renegade breaking all the rules specializing in buying small-market publications with fewer than 50,000 subscribers in circulation and turning them into literary forces to be reckoned with. He was a self-proclaimed tyrant, an oracle of publishing, arrogant but with a long line of successful newspapers to support his claims. The core principle of his business model was to inflict his distinctive style on every paper he owned. Hands-on in all of his ventures, Burt had moved to St. Killian to evaluate the *Palmchat Gazette* and ensure it was functioning to his satisfaction and specifications.

The reputation of the surly publisher had everyone at the newspaper anxious, except Vivian. She was reeling and off-kilter for an entirely different reason. One that had nothing to do with the man's demanding and critical editing style or his penchant for drastically cutting expenses through workforce reductions. Vivian had been stunned because Burt Bronson reconnected her with the past she was trying to forget. He was the one link to the man she was still madly in love with—his son, Leo.

Chapter Six

One day Vivian would see Leo again and feel nothing.

Too bad that day hadn't been last night.

The street circus had been epic, an experience she would never forget. The air had been charged with frenetic electricity. Bodies gyrated to calypso music as circus performers weaved through the crowd, thrilling onlookers with their acrobatic prowess. A massive stage, an island in the middle of the street intersection, displayed aerial acts including tightrope walkers, trampoline tumblers, and trapeze artists.

Vivian sighed, remembering the moment when she'd paused from dancing with one of the street clowns to grab a plastic cup filled to the brim with Felipe beer and noticed Amal was no longer dancing beside her. Flushed and panting, she'd pushed her way through the throngs looking for Amal. With the record crowd flooding the streets, it had been an impossible mission. Giving up, Vivian decided to text her to find out where she was.

Just as she grabbed her phone, it vibrated in her hand. On the screen was a text message from Amal: *Found my waiter, gonna get laid tonight. See ya manana!*

Her best friend was notorious for disappearing to run off and hook up with locals on vacation. Vivian just wished Amal hadn't picked Landon George. Despite the warnings she'd given her best friend about him, Vivian couldn't deny that the man was as sexy as it got and that was the only criteria Amal ever used.

Stuffing her phone back into the front pocket of her cross-body purse, Vivian squeezed through the sweaty bodies in the street intersection. Thirty minutes later, she ducked down a side street to the back of one of the bars where a small wooden deck extended into the sand facing the water. The cool breeze wafting off the sea caressed her skin, giving her goose bumps. Vivian closed her eyes and breathed in deeply, allowing the ocean air to fill her lungs.

"Well, aren't you a sight for sore eyes."

The baritone voice she would never forget had stunned her as she opened her eyes and focused on the stars, scattered across the onyx sky. Vivian fought the urge to turn around and face the man behind her. Her emotions in turmoil, she struggled to stifle the longing to do something she'd regret later.

As a jolt of excitement flooded through her veins, resignation settled in. Tonight, restraint would lose the fight. Turning slowly, she saw the love of her life standing in front of her, too close and yet not close enough. His piercing, clear blue eyes bore into hers communicating a passion she'd seen only in her dreams over the past year and a half.

Words were exchanged in a blur, snatches of sentences her mind couldn't quite remember. She could still feel the sensation of his mouth, his tongue whipping and swirling around hers. His hand slipped beneath the hem of her short mini-dress and then trailed up the inside of her thigh. Her body throbbed in anticipation of what she knew was to come, what she was craving, what she had to have again, even if it was just for one night.

His fingers had explored her, bringing her close but not over the edge, before entering her completely, with ardent force. He entered her inch by inch, slowly at first, before quickening his pace in a frenzied rhythm, awakening nerve endings and sending her into a spasm of deep tremors of ecstasy. The crowd singing loudly along with the circus musicians to popular island songs drowned out her moans.

The squawk of the seagull landing back on the balcony railing shook Vivian from her memories. Her skin flushed, she wanted nothing more than to feel Leo pulsating within her again. Right now. The man was like a drug. Vivian felt a tear escape from her eye. How had she allowed herself to be seduced so easily by the man who'd trashed her heart? Her breakup with Leo had sent her into a dizzying downward spiral that annihilated her life and everything she thought she knew about herself.

"Shoo, bird, I got nothing for you," Vivian said as she waved a hand at the bird, sending him flying off toward the aquamarine water, its waves shimmering with a tint of gold from the bright sun.

Wiping the tears from her face, Vivian walked toward the chaise and sat down. Amal still wasn't back from her vacation sex, and Vivian had no one to commiserate with about her sexcapade last night. Fluffing the pillows behind her, she leaned back and gazed out at the water. Two sailboats were anchored off shore. Jet skiers zigzagged through the boats in concert with the fragments of thoughts shifting through her mind.

All the credit for the distance after their split rested solely with Vivian. She'd walked out on Leo, leaving nothing more than a "Dear John" letter to explain her abrupt absence.

The breakup itself was orchestrated by Leo alone. Five words uttered from Leo's lips had done more than just end their relationship. It had devastated her entire life. Everything she thought she'd wanted had lost its appeal. The high of gallivanting across the African continent exposing political corruption and atrocities had gone from righteous and uplifting to sad and disheartening.

With five little words, she'd grown dissatisfied with the life they'd built working side by side as investigative reporters. The microcosm of her life had changed, and she couldn't get away fast enough. She'd flown halfway around the world, shocking her editor with her resignation from *The Washington Post* before slinking off to her mother's winter home in Aspen. Depression had descended upon her, and she became a recluse, shunning her family and friends for months as she struggled to make sense of her disillusionment.

Five words had triggered it all.

I don't believe in marriage.

Leo was matter-of-fact and unapologetic when he'd first said those words to Vivian as if he was speaking of leprechauns or unicorns.

As much of a nonconformist as she was professionally, personally, Vivian was a traditionalist. She was proud of her desire to get married to an amazing man and raise children with him. She'd been devastated to learn, after five years of a monogamous, committed relationship founded on passionate love, that marriage was off the table for Leo and children weren't even on the radar. He resolutely refused to entertain the ideas, and Vivian still didn't understand why.

Leo had insisted that his views on marriage had nothing to do with his unconditional love for her or their relationship. She was the only woman he'd ever loved, and she would be the only one he loved for the rest of his life. Despite his reassurances, Vivian couldn't help but feel as though there was something wrong with her. Why was this man who professed to love her so much unwilling to marry her?

Unable to accept the divergent beliefs she and Leo had about marriage, a line had been drawn in the sand the day she ran away, one neither she nor Leo could erase. Making love under the moon and stars on a Caribbean night would never be enough to bridge the chasm between them.

Chapter Seven

The high-end luxury outdoor mall was about a mile from Vivian's condo complex, along a meandering sidewalk, offering unobstructed views of a shallow pink sand beach littered with seashells and lined with tall palm trees. Vivian had grown tired of waiting for Amal to return or even respond to her many texts and voice messages. She'd needed a distraction from Leo. The next best thing to a tongue lashing from her best friend was retail therapy.

Heat wafted from the pavement, creating an outdoor sauna effect. Vivian regretted walking back with all her bags under the bright sun as sweat slid down her face to her neck and chest. Her braids clung to her damp skin, making her body temperature rise even higher. As the handles of her bags sent sharp stings into her left hand, Vivian paused to readjust them onto her shoulder.

Shopping initially hadn't provided the respite she wanted. The realization that Leo was somewhere on this island had panicked Vivian, making her antsy and nervous. Her heart longed to call him and find out why he was here, although she suspected it had something to do with the massive heart attack his father had suffered six months ago. Why hadn't Burt called to warn her that Leo was on the island?

Knowing Burt as she did now, he probably withheld the information for her own good. Trying to talk to Leo again was futile. Vivian didn't want to subject herself to the same heartache she'd gone through after coming home from Africa. Last night was just a minor setback, and nothing that had transpired between her and Leo as they made love on the beach could magically change Leo's views on marriage. There was no future for her and Leo. She wouldn't allow herself to continue to love and commit herself to a man who was unwilling to make the ultimate commitment to her. She was worth more than what Leo was willing to give.

As she walked through the wrought iron gates of the condo complex, Vivian heard a familiar, cheerful cadence.

"Vivian! Welcome back. How was your shopping?" Mr. Percy Higginbottom, the elderly property manager, emerged from the management office, waving his hands frantically.

"As you can see, I contributed quite a lot to the St. Killian economy this afternoon," Vivian said, turning to show him the bags hanging from her left shoulder.

"Indeed you did," said Mr. Higginbottom, a big smile spreading across his round face. "I saw your beautiful friend this morning, the one with the long black hair."

"This morning?" Vivian frowned. She hadn't left for the mall until the afternoon. If Amal had returned this morning, why hadn't she come back to the condo?

"Yes, I was out here trying to capture sand crabs. For some reason, they are particularly bad this year. As you know, it is against the island law to kill the little critters. I must carefully lure them into a shoe box and transport them back to the beach. A painstaking process."

Smiling, Vivian sat her bags on the ground. "Did you let my friend into my condo?"

"Oh no! I would never let anyone into your condo. That is

against property management rules." Mr. Higginbottom shook his head vigorously.

"It's okay. Remember, I told you she's my best friend from high school. She's staying with me for the next week." Vivian placed a hand on his arm, trying to calm him down. "Where is she now?"

"Who?"

"My friend that you saw this morning ..." Vivian raised an eyebrow.

"Yes, your friend! She told me to give you a message, and I promised her I would, just as soon as I finished gathering a few of the sand crabs. My eyesight isn't what it used to be, you know. I caught about five, but in my younger years, I would catch twenty to fifty a day!"

"I see." Vivian nodded slowly and then asked, "Mr. Higginbottom, what was the message my friend wanted you to give me?"

"Yes, she wanted you to know that she was going on an overnight excursion to St. Mateo with her special friend and that her cell phone battery was dead. Or maybe that she wouldn't get reception out on the sea. I can't remember. But she left a note! Let me go grab it for you, wait here."

Vivian placed a hand on her hip. Amal had planned to visit her so they could hang out like old times, and less than six hours into the trip, she had disappeared for the night and planned to be gone for another day and night.

Looking at her watch, she saw it had been almost twenty minutes since Mr. Higginbottom had gone to fetch the note. She wondered what was taking him so long. After another minute had passed, Vivian peered toward the small window of the office building, seeing no activity.

Stepping over her bags, she headed for the door and turned the knob. Vivian pushed the door open slightly and saw the elderly man playing solitaire on his computer. What was going on? Had he even looked for the note?

"Excuse me," Vivian said, making a concerted effort to control her annoyance. "Did you find the note from my friend?"

"Oh my, no, I couldn't find it," Mr. Higginbottom said, as he hastily lifted a few of the piles of paper on his desk. "I will keep looking for it and let you know as soon as I locate it. It has to be here somewhere."

Vivian sighed heavily. "Okay, thank you."

Pulling the door shut behind her, she thought the likelihood of him finding Amal's note was slim to none.

Chapter Eight

By the time Vivian turned down the narrow sidewalk toward her condo, she was drenched in sweat. Dragging the three bags filled with a thousand dollars' worth of clothes, Vivian lamented the time wasted with Mr. Higginbottom. Her frustration was not the old man's fault. He hadn't made her best friend ditch her for some "good D" as Amal would say. If she was honest though, her ill temper had nothing to do with Mr. Higginbottom or Amal and everything to do with Leo.

Vivian lengthened her strides and grabbed her keys from the front pocket of her jeans, anxious to get inside the cool air-conditioned condo. Angry yelps from her neighbor's dog grew louder with each step. Something had agitated the mild-mannered Yorkie. Vivian couldn't remember a time when the dog had barked this intensely before.

"Shh, it's okay." Vivian tried to soothe the dog, as she sat her bags down in front of the door. Through the gaps in the wooden fence surrounding the courtyard, Vivian could see the Yorkie pacing back and forth. Inching closer, she peered through the slats and saw no signs the dog was hurt. Maybe the dog was just hungry and upset from being left behind. She could relate to that. Vivian hoped her neighbor would return soon. She was in no mood to hear the dog barking for much longer.

Walking back toward her door, Vivian held the key out to place it in the keyhole and paused. Her hand began to tremble.

The door was slightly ajar.

Had she opened it before checking on the dog? Could she have forgotten to close it before she left?

Pushing the door in slightly with her right hand, Vivian peeked through the opening. Nothing looked disturbed in her living room. Vivian took a small step forward. Her eyes roamed over the kitchen and dining room. Nothing was out of place. Distracted by thoughts of Leo, she might not have closed the door completely when she left.

Grabbing her bags, she crossed the threshold, sat them on the couch, and then closed the door behind her. Vivian took off her tank top and stood in the middle of the room, allowing the cool air to embrace her skin. Walking over to the refrigerator, she grabbed a bottle of water before checking her cell phone again for a message from Amal. Vivian wasn't sure if she could trust Mr. Higginbottom's memory. The man was befuddled at best and absentminded at worst. Amal's cell phone could be dead, but she expected her industrious friend to have bought a replacement charger by now to allow them to keep in touch. Or maybe Landon's sexual prowess was just that good that Amal didn't care about abandoning her best friend for a couple of days.

Vivian smiled at the thought. There was a time she would have done the same thing for Leo.

Taking a couple of gulps from the water bottle, Vivian leaned on the counter. Memories of Leo began to flood her mind. She'd been ashamed by what she'd allowed last night.

Basking in the aftershocks of making love on the lounge chair behind the bar, Vivian had allowed herself to go back in time as Leo's arms wrapped around her. Everything had been perfect between them for almost five years. Simply loving each other had been enough. When had that stopped being enough for her? Why couldn't she accept Leo's love without the condition of marriage? Was the piece of paper worth walking away from the man she still loved after all this time?

Confused by her wayward thoughts, she'd pushed away from Leo, slipping back into her dress before running off along the beach back to her parked car. She could hear him calling her name as he struggled to find his clothes, but it was too late.

Her heart and her mind were aligned. She refused to be in a stagnant relationship. She deserved better. She deserved a man who wanted to marry her and have a family and—

A loud thud followed by a sharp bang against a wall jolted Vivian.

Reaching down to the floor, Vivian scooped up her tank top and put it on. Her breathing ragged and rushed, she stood still listening for another sound.

Was someone upstairs in her condo? Was that why the little dog was barking like crazy? Was there a burglar in her home? Looking to her right, Vivian picked up the first heavy object she saw in the kitchen, a wooden rolling pin. Not the best weapon, but her hands were shaking hard.

What happened to the woman who'd hunted down African warlords, brandishing an AK-47 for protection, just to get a quote for her next exposé? She would never have felt this trepidation two years ago. Vivian was known for plunging into dangerous situations without thinking, much to Leo's dismay. The casual, laid-back island life had dulled her instincts and her pursuit of danger. She didn't trust herself to wield a knife at the moment.

Heart pounding, she took a few steps, careful not to make any noise on the travertine tile floor. Maybe she was just hearing things.

Or could Amal have returned? One of the maintenance workers

might have let her inside. Easing toward the staircase, Vivian stopped for a moment to steady her breathing.

Another loud thud made her heart jump into her throat.

Someone was upstairs.

Slowly ascending the staircase, Vivian reached the top of the landing faster than she wanted. She should call the cops instead of trying to play amateur sleuth, but the reporter in her was too curious not to investigate.

Staying close to the wall, she could see the den was empty, but the glass pocket doors to her balcony were opened slightly. Vivian was certain she'd closed those before leaving. Holding the rolling pin above her head, Vivian took small steps toward the edge of the wall next to the hallway separating her guest bedrooms from the study. With a quick glance around the corner, she saw a light on in one of the guest bedrooms.

But not the one Amal was staying in.

This bedroom was used for storing unpacked boxes filled with items Vivian couldn't remember and probably didn't need.

As she turned the corner and inched down the hallway toward the bedroom door, Vivian heard more banging and rustling inside. Blood rushed through her ears, muffling the sound, and her body shook with each step.

Wanting to make sure it wasn't Amal, she thought of calling out to her best friend, but the words stuck in her throat.

She was too afraid.

Abandoning her original resolve, Vivian took a step backward. A figure emerged from the room dressed in all black.

Screaming, Vivian turned to run down the stairs. As she took the steps two at a time, she heard a soft feminine scream merge with her own. Pausing at the bottom of the stairs, Vivian looked behind her to see her maid, Cozette.

"Ms. Vivian, you scared me so bad!"

"Cozette! What the hell are you doing here?" Vivian asked.

"Remember, I asked if I could come clean for you this weekend instead of during the week because of my family reunion. Everybody's coming to the island tomorrow, and I'll be too busy with our activities ..." Cozette said, a worried look on her face.

Vivian let out a sigh and leaned against the wall. "I completely forgot about that. I'm sorry, Cozette."

"No, I'm sorry, Ms. Vivian. I should have reminded you." Cozette gave a nervous laugh and placed her hand on the wall to steady herself. "I thought you were a burglar trying to bash my head in with that rolling pin."

Vivian smiled with relief. "What were you doing in there?"

"I saw the box labeled exercise equipment. I was going to move it to your new workout room. I was moving the boxes to get to that one. I'm sorry I was loud, some of them were really heavy," Cozette said.

"I understand." The mystery was solved.

"Is it okay for me to finish cleaning?"

"Yes, of course. And, Cozette, be careful coming in next time. You left the front door ajar."

Chapter Nine

Leaving the kitchen with two mugs of steaming fresh-brewed coffee, Vivian ventured upstairs to Amal's guest room, anxious to get the salacious, sordid details about her best friend's extended one-night stand.

Heading down the hallway, Vivian debated whether or not she would divulge the salacious, sordid details of her secret dalliance. Vivian still couldn't believe she'd hooked up with Leo at the street circus. What had she been thinking? Well, she knew the answer to that question. She hadn't been thinking. She'd been too wrapped up in her emotions, too caught up in Leo and the electric, mesmerizing effects he still held over her. Time apart had definitely made her heart grow fonder. Leo was as sexy and irresistible as ever, and she had been unable to push him away. As soon as she'd heard his voice, all rational thought had fled, leaving behind an eagerness to succumb to his touch.

Vivian had berated herself for her recklessness, and yet, part of her didn't regret the encounter. Still, as she knocked on Amal's door, Vivian knew she wasn't ready to spill her secrets to her best friend. Nine o'clock on a Sunday morning was too early for blunt, tough love.

"Amal?" Vivian put one of the mugs on a narrow console table positioned against the wall and then opened the door.

Amal wasn't in her room.

The bright sun shone through the windows, illuminating the emptiness, made even more disappointing by the unmade bed.

More than a bit annoyed, Vivian took the coffee back to the kitchen, wondering where the hell Amal could be. Three sips of coffee later, Vivian abandoned the java, remembering the note from Amal Mr. Higginbottom had told her about, anxious to read it.

Changing from her pajama shorts and a camisole into khaki shorts and a camo-printed tank, Vivian tied her long, flowing braids back into a ponytail, shoved her feet into the pair of deck shoes she kept near the front door, and left the condo.

Vivian hurried along the winding path to the property manager's office, curious about why Amal hadn't called to check in with her. Vivian wasn't her best friend's keeper, but a quick text from Amal would have put Vivian's mind at ease. Amal's prolonged absence didn't really upset her, though. Her best friend had pulled disappearing acts before, seeking various and sundry "vacation sex" experiences.

What bothered Vivian was Amal's hookup with Landon George. Thinking of her best friend with the shifty crook worried Vivian; she couldn't shake the apprehension.

The waiter seemed to be, at the most, a petty wannabe criminal, but was that just an act? Thinking back on her interview with Landon, she remembered thinking his protests of innocence weren't just deceptive but deliberate. Like the African warlords she'd interrogated, the waiter had given her disinformation. She'd left the meeting with Landon feeling as though she'd been talking to the mastermind, not just a minion.

As she neared the property manager's office, Vivian chided herself for worrying. Amal was savvy, clever, and tough. A badass boss bitch. She resided among the pampered elite in Palm Beach now, but Amal had survived, and thrived, in a tough urban neighborhood. Amal could take care of herself.

"Yes, I have the note right here," said Mr. Higginbottom, after Vivian had entered his office and reminded him about his promise to find the note from Amal. Moving behind his desk, littered with papers, folders, brochures, and pamphlets, he put on a pair of glasses and began shuffling through the several small mounds.

"Here it is," he announced, peering at the piece of paper he'd unearthed. "Oh, no, wait, this is not it. This is a note to remind myself to call my cousin's neighbor, Mrs. White. Her godson works at the Purple Gecko, where they found the hit-and-run victim. Nasty business. Did you write that story?"

"No, I didn't." Vivian shook her head and then cleared her throat. "Mr. Higginbottom, you said you had the note from my friend. Can you please find it?"

"Oh, yes, of course," said the man as he fished through his sea of haphazard papers and excavated another piece of paper, proclaiming it as the note from Amal. "Here you are!"

"Thanks," Vivian mumbled, unable to mask her frustration as she read the note. "Mr. Higginbottom, this note is not from my friend."

"I beg your pardon?"

"This note says: Met a great guy and we're going on a sunset cruise. Don't wait up. I'll be back tomorrow for breakfast. Sally," Vivian said, her frustration escalating to annoyance.

"Sally isn't your friend?" Mr. Higginbottom asked, confusion in his owl-like eyes. "Are you sure? The beautiful girl with the long dark hair and gray eyes like a summer storm?"

"Amal's eyes aren't gray," Vivian said, her disappointment giving way to a strange despair. "I don't know anyone named Sally."

"Neither do I," said the office manager, shaking his head.

"However, there is something I do know, or rather, something I remember!"

Not amused by the elder man's befuddled temperament, Vivian asked, "What?"

"I remember your friend!" Mr. Higginbottom exclaimed. "She's the lovely woman from Egypt, right?"

Vivian crossed her arms, irritated. "Did you talk to her?"

"I actually did more than that," pronounced Mr. Higginbottom, with pride. "Your friend, if I remember correctly, and I do believe I am at the moment. Although, sometimes, my memory, which once was better than that of an elephant—"

"Mr. Higginbottom, please," implored Vivian. "Tell me what happened with Amal."

"Oh, yes, right! Well, you see," began the property manager, somewhat conspiratorially, "your friend came to me needing assistance with calling a cab, and I told her that I would do no such thing! I informed her that I would be very offended if she didn't allow me to drive her where she needed to go, and so—"

"Wait a minute," Vivian said, holding up a hand to stop him. "You drove Amal somewhere?"

"Indeed I did," said Mr. Higginbottom. "I was happy to do it because I was anxious to ask her questions about Egypt, which is one of the places my Martha has always dreamed of going, but your friend was very distracted and seemed preoccupied with her thoughts, so I wasn't able to get much from her about the pyramids and ancient ruins and—"

"Where did you take Amal?" Vivian demanded.

"She requested that I drive her to the Palmchat Rides and Rentals," said the property manager. "It's a rental car company near downtown."

Skeptical, Vivian asked, "What time was this?"

"Why, if I remember correctly, it was around ten o'clock," said the older man.

"You took her to a rental car company at ten o'clock at night?" Vivian asked. "And the place was still open?"

"I believe it was," he said, looking at the ceiling for a moment and then back at her. "I mean, I think so. Unless it was ten o'clock in the morning. But, no, that couldn't be right because my program comes on at eleven o'clock and I can't miss it, so I wouldn't have been able to—"

"Was it one of the rental car companies at the airport?" Vivian asked. Most of the major rental companies had offices at the St. Killian International Airport and had extended hours to accommodate travelers who often arrived on the island after midnight. Palmchat Rides seemed local, but maybe they had an office near the airport.

"Oh, no, I didn't take her to the airport," said Mr. Higginbottom. "She wanted to rent a car, you see. She wasn't trying to catch a flight."

Vexed by his muddled information, which she realized she couldn't count on, Vivian thanked the man for his time and exited his office.

Ten minutes later, back at the condo, Vivian stood in the small courtyard. Covered by an awning which blocked the sun, the area was accessed from a door at the rear of the attached garage. It was quaint and cozy. It had bistro tables and potted hibiscus plants, and the ground was pea gravel and flagstone.

Vivian stared at a hibiscus flower. Its bright yellow petals fluttered in the balmy breeze.

Amal's behavior was at once confusing, annoying, and troubling. Vivian didn't know if her conflicted feelings demanded action, but the investigative reporter in her wanted answers. Had Amal rented a car? If so, why? Amal didn't need her own car. Vivian was more than happy to play chauffeur.

Vivian tried to remember what time she'd lost sight of Amal at the street circus but then recalled the text Amal had sent her about hooking up with Landon. Back inside, Vivian grabbed her cell phone from the purse she'd deposited on the breakfast bar and searched for the text.

After finding it, she focused on the time Amal had sent it—11:16 p.m. Mr. Higginbottom claimed he'd driven Amal to the rental car company around 10:00 p.m., which would have been an hour before Amal's text. Why would Amal ask the property manager to drive her to a rental car company and then, an hour later, send a text to Vivian about hooking up with Landon? Had Amal driven the rental car to meet Landon somewhere? But, why rent a car when Amal could have easily taken a cab to hook up with the waiter?

Vivian shook her head. Speculation was pointless. She needed the truth, and one person could provide answers. Landon George. But, would the waiter be honest with her? Or, as he had when she'd questioned him before, would Landon try to deceive her with misdirection and misinformation?

Chapter Ten

Vivian looked over at Landon, who was arranging fruit in the buffet display. He paused to run a hand over his golden-tipped dreadlocks, stealing a glance in her direction, and then moved with frenetic accuracy arranging the diced fruit into an artful display.

Vivian needed to find a way to get this damn waiter to talk to her. The history between her and Landon was strained, causing him to be aloof and suspicious. He'd sneered at her before blowing off her initial inquiries. Dismissively, he told her that he met thousands of tourists every day and it was impossible for him to remember them all. Vivian hadn't been deterred, demanding to know the details of his conversation with Amal during lunch two days ago. Not intimidated, the waiter had given her flippant ignorance, which infuriated her even more.

"Just remember, you can catch more flies with honey." Leo's words floated through Vivian's mind, a remnant of an encounter from their past.

The first time they'd met was at the beginning of a three-day cruise of Lake Nasser between southern Egypt and northern Sudan. She had seen him on the upper deck of the boat, looking out at the desert. The breeze ruffled through his mass of unruly chestnut-brown curls. His scruffy beard gave him a ruggedness, masking the classic American boy-next-door look, and accentuated his mesmerizing blue eyes.

Leo had caught her staring at him, and a pink blush had spread over her golden fawn-colored skin. Walking over to her, he'd flashed her a brilliant smile before striking up an innocent conversation. He'd been engaging, delighting her with easy, casual, often flirty banter.

The attraction had been instantaneous between them. Vivian couldn't contain the onslaught of lascivious thoughts as Leo gave her his undivided attention. Her body craved a passionate connection with his as her lust spiraled out of control. But Leo had other things in mind. Seduction of her body wasn't his primary goal.

Despite the outward manifestation of her attraction to him, Leo had seen through it all to her real reason for being on the cruise. Piercing her defenses, he'd picked up on the pensiveness and frustration she felt as she worked on her first story for *The Washington Post*. She'd been trying for weeks to figure out how to get the doctor of the Zimbabwe dictator to talk to her. Puzzled, but intrigued, Leo had asked Vivian why she would want to talk to a dictator's doctor? She'd explained how she was a new reporter and needed the interview to finish her article before the deadline, which was fast approaching.

Giving her that one nugget of advice, the first of many, Leo had explained that "honey" was a tactic he often employed when he was having problems securing an interview. Vivian had looked at him shrewdly, guessing what he'd failed to reveal—Leo was also a reporter on assignment in Africa. Confessing his profession as a journalist for *The New York Times*, Leo had given her a sheepish smile, melting her heart and her initial instinct to be upset with him for his omission.

Leo suggested she present her request to the doctor as a profile of his life and work, an ode to his contributions to the people of

Zimbabwe. Then, he advised that she subtly introduce a few questions about the dictator and his alleged money laundering. Vivian had thought Leo was brilliant, solving her conundrum with such simplicity.

The following days on the cruise, Leo had found clever ways to get her to spend all of her time with him. Vivian soon realized his interest in her was deep, more spiritual and mental than physical. As they explored the ancient temples of Amada, Derr, and the Tomb of Penout, their connection was undeniable and different from any relationship Vivian had had in the past. Their conversations had become more serious, as Leo explored the depths of her thoughts and feelings on all manners of subjects. Vivian found herself drawn to him like she hadn't been to any man before. She loved the way he made love to her mind before making any attempts to conquer her body.

She and Leo had been in sync from that very first trip. They were the perfect complements to each other, his calmness balancing her feistiness. The supportive and nurturing relationship they later developed was a testament to their first encounter. She and Leo were a formidable team. Vivian wished he was with her right now, helping her to break through Landon's wall. Leo would know exactly what to do. He was the yin to her yang, seeing the forest when she was so busy looking at the trees.

Vivian forced the memories from her mind. Leo would not be swooping in to guide her this time. She had no clue where he was on the island or if he was still around. Hoping for his presence was a waste of time, but that didn't mean he couldn't help her. She'd tried the aggressive, tough approach on Landon with no success. Maybe, it was time to try some of Leo's honey.

Chapter Eleven

"I'm sorry for my behavior earlier," Vivian began, studying Landon's handsome face for any sign he'd be more forthcoming with information. The waiter sat across from her at one of the small tables toward the back of the restaurant. His dark eyes were a bit softer now, after she'd approached him more contrite and asked if he'd be willing to talk to her for just five minutes. Vivian had been surprised he agreed.

Landon didn't respond, waiting for her to continue.

Sliding her cell phone across the table to him, Vivian showed a picture of a happy Amal from two nights ago, looking stunning in her red strapless sundress and matching red scarf draped over her shoulders.

"This is my best friend, Amal," Vivian said. "I've known her since we were fourteen years old, and she's probably the person that I'm closest to on this planet. We love each other like sisters."

Landon reached over and lifted the screen, squinting at the photo, a hint of a smile sneaking toward the corners of his mouth.

Vivian continued, "She came here to spend a week with me, and I haven't seen her in almost two days, since the first night of the street circus. I'm starting to get worried about her. I got a text from her a little after eleven that night saying that she'd found you and the two of you were going out. And, I haven't heard from her since."

Vivian was surprised by the emotions creeping into her voice as she spoke, a sign of the secret fears she hadn't let herself acknowledge.

"Do you know what happened to her? Do you know where she is right now?"

"Wait a minute now, I didn't do anything to anyone," Landon said, shifting in his chair as he dropped the cell phone onto the table.

"I'm not saying that you did anything to her. But, you may be the last person who saw her that night. Did you meet up with her?"

"Look, I do remember your friend," Landon said, an appreciative look on his face as he crossed his arms over his chest.

Vivian sighed, "Okay, do you remember her from lunch or from later that night? I'm not trying to get you in trouble, Landon; I just need to find my friend. I'm concerned that she may need help, and I have to figure out what's going on with her."

Squinting, Landon looked at Vivian as if contemplating his next move.

"She told me she was meeting up with you Friday night for a date."

"A date? In my dreams," Landon said, shaking his head. "No, we had a business transaction that evening."

"A business transaction? Are you sure?" Vivian scowled.

"The only thing going on between me and your friend was business. But I would have preferred it to be a date," Landon said, a hint of mischief in his tone. "She is a stunningly beautiful woman. I never met no Egyptian woman before. Exquisite."

"So, the two of you didn't hook up?" Vivian asked, remembering what Amal had texted her.

Found my waiter, gonna get laid tonight. See ya manana!

"Believe it or not, I do have other talents." Landon let out a low chuckle and raised an eyebrow.

"What other talents was my friend interested in?"

"I have been known to procure items for guests to the island. Things that are hard to come by. It is a service that I do gladly, for a fee, of course."

"She paid you money to get an item for her?" Vivian asked.

"She paid extra for same-day service. Plus, she gave me a nice tip, too. Beautiful and generous she was."

"I don't understand." Vivian felt her chest tightening as she tried to make sense of Landon's admission. "What did you get for her?"

Landon leaned forward across the table, reducing the space between Vivian and himself. Trailing a finger along the side of her arm, he said slowly, "My clients pay me for discretion."

Vivian bristled at his touch, anger radiating through her body as she realized his new angle. "How much is it going to cost me?"

"I don't know. How much is your best friend worth to you?"

A chill ran down Vivian's spine as she realized Landon was toying with her. Had he met up with Amal that night or was he just using her concern for her best friend to his advantage to get extra money in his pocket? Vivian couldn't take a chance. She had to find out what he knew and then try to validate the information later.

"I only have five hundred dollars on me right now—"

"That works fine."

Vivian pulled out her wallet, grabbing the five bills from her purse and placed them into Landon's outstretched hand.

"Amal wanted a special item that would take a few hours to procure," Landon began, his tone professional. "I tracked it down through a few of my friends and called her when I'd located it. She was at the street carnival at the time and asked me to come pick her up. I texted her when I arrived, and I saw her when she slipped away from you. You were too busy grinding on that street clown to even notice."

Vivian rolled her eyes, wishing Landon would get on with it.

"We left, and I drove her to a business partner of mine to get her what she requested."

"Landon, just tell me what she bought, please."

"A Glock nine millimeter."

Chapter Twelve

Gripping the steering wheel, Vivian drove like a madwoman speeding along the narrow island roads, using the GPS on her phone for navigation. Landon's reluctant confession reverberated through her mind. Every cell in her body had immediately rejected his version of events. Vivian knew Amal better than anyone. They were as close as sisters, sharing everything with each other since they first met in the library on the first day of school in ninth grade.

She'd seen Amal at her best and her worst over their fifteen-year friendship. Not once had Amal shown an interest or a need for a gun.

Amal's trip to St. Killian was a chance for them to hang out again after not seeing each other in person for almost two years. Not some dangerous or clandestine mission. Landon had to be lying, she'd thought.

She was wrong.

Her resolve to convict Landon as a liar crumbled as his story continued. After Amal had bought the nine-millimeter Glock, she'd asked Landon to drop her off at a rental car facility, Palmchat Rides and Rentals. The same facility Mr. Higginbottom told Vivian he'd taken Amal to. Landon had refused but offered to take her to Vivian's condo which was on the way to his after-hours gig as a DJ at a local nightclub. He'd dropped her off shortly before ten that night.

A sickening realization had settled over Vivian. A dizzying collection of puzzle pieces melded together unexpectedly. Landon's excursion with Amal corroborated what she'd learned from Mr. Higginbottom, both in action and timeline. The similarities were impossible to ignore.

Could she have missed the signs that Amal was in trouble?

Since her break up with Leo a year and a half ago, Vivian had been distant and distracted, consumed with avoiding her emotional turmoil by throwing herself into her new island life. She'd shunned everything from the past five years and even avoided Amal for a while, embarrassed to discuss the downfall of the epic love she'd gone on and on about with her before. Amal had been supportive, knowing when Vivian needed space and, later, when she needed comfort and a sympathetic ear. In all that time, had she been so self-involved not to realize that her best friend was dealing with a conflict of her own? Dread seeped through Vivian's pores. She needed to do what she did best. Follow the leads of this story and find her best friend, before it was too late.

About thirty minutes and several wrong turns later, Vivian turned the Range Rover into what looked like a used car lot with a hodgepodge of vehicles crammed on either side of a squat building constructed of corrugated metal siding. Steering the SUV around a minivan and a hatchback, Vivian inched into an empty space in front of the plate glass façade.

Chimes from bells attached to the door announced her entrance, as she walked into the small building.

"Hey beautiful lady!" A small, squat St. Killian man called out, giving Vivian a broad grin, his tone promising a hard sell. "How can I help you? What kind of ride you looking for? I got just what you need, something fast and sexy? A red convertible?"

"Actually," Vivian said, slightly nauseated by the smell of rubber, car exhaust and cheap cologne permeating the air, "I'm looking for some information and hopefully you can help."

"What kind of information? Are you lost? You need a map of the island?"

"I need to ask you a few questions," Vivian said, trying not to be discouraged by the doubt in his piercing gaze.

"What kind of questions?" He asked, decidedly more wary and less ingratiating as he eyed her suspiciously.

"You have GPS tracking devices on the cars you rent?"

Eyes narrowed, he asked, "Why you want to know that?"

"I'm looking for my friend." Vivian placed her cell phone on the counter, tapping the screen to reveal a picture of Amal. "Her name is Amal Shahin. I think she rented a car from you and I need to know if you can help me find her. Please. This is what she looks like. Do you recognize her?"

The owner's eyes narrowed as he peered at the cell phone screen. "Maybe. I don't know. Look, I have a business to run. Don't got no time to be interrogated."

"I'm not trying to interrogate you," Vivian said. "I just want to know the location of the car my friend rented."

"Can't give out that information," he said. "If you can't find your friend, you need to call the cops."

"I'll pay you," Vivian blurted out, opening her purse. "Tell me what I need to know and I'll give you a hundred bucks."

"You got to understand my position. You say this lady who rented the car is your friend, but how do I know that is true? Maybe you trying to find her because you want to do her some harm? I tell you where the car is, you go there, hurt this lady, it's gonna be my fault."

"Two hundred," Vivian said, feeling desperate and frustrated.

"Two hundred fifty." He countered, his eyes shrewd. "And a free ad in the paper."

Confused, Vivian stared at him. "What?"

"You that lady reporter at the Palmchat Gazette, ain't you?" He asked. "Thought I recognized you. I seen that little picture of you next to your name."

Rolling her eyes at the man's avarice, Vivian conceded. "Fine. Now, tell me where I can find the car that my friend rented."

Chapter Thirteen

"The Purple Gecko?" Vivian shook her head. The place was a dump. Constructed of concrete and weathered clapboard, the bar had the same dimensions as a double-wide trailer with a lone pneumatic screen door as the entry point. Located in Handweg Gardens, the neighborhood was dangerous, even in the daytime. A gun would be a necessary precaution for wandering this area late at night. Was that why Amal bought the gun? Why did she come to this neighborhood? Was she going to the Purple Gecko?

Shifting gears, Vivian drove across the crushed pebble of the parking lot to a dirt road next to the side of the building. The small black Corolla Amal had rented was parked near a row of banana trees near the back of the bar. Using the company's GPS software, the owner of Palmchat Rides and Rentals was able to track the car Amal had rented, pinpointing its location. The car had been in the same location for the past two days, near a dead end on Sandy Coral Road.

Judging the distance from the car to the bar, it would have been a short five-minute walk. No one at the bar would have been able to see the car sitting on the side, obscured by the surrounding trees. Like hiding in plain sight. Had Amal planned it this way? Was she hiding from someone? Or following someone?

Vivian shifted the Range Rover into park and leaned toward the steering wheel, peering through the windshield. Maybe the car was stolen, and the thief drove it here, for whatever reason, and then abandoned it. The thought of Amal being carjacked late at night was even more disturbing than her purchasing a gun.

Pushing those wayward thoughts from her mind, Vivian stepped out of the Range Rover and walked toward the black Corolla. The car was probably locked. Vivian had a feeling this little sleuthing expedition was going to be a bust, but she had to follow it through. Her frustration was growing, making her desperate for any clear sign of Amal's whereabouts. She had to keep searching until she found something concrete. Something that led to Amal.

Glancing over her shoulder, Vivian took quick steps to the driver's side door of the black compact. Resting her hand on the door handle, Vivian gripped it gently and pulled.

The car door opened.

Making a quick check toward the empty parking lot, Vivian saw no one around. No one watching her.

She sat in the driver's seat and looked around the interior of the car. It was spotless. No objects and no sign that Amal, or anyone for that matter, had been inside the vehicle. Vivian opened the middle console and the glove compartment. Both empty. Damn it!

Taking a deep breath, Vivian leaned back against the seat and fought to control the panic rising in her gut. The car had been her last chance to get information on Amal's location, and it was turning into a dead end. There were no more clues for her to follow. No other leads that could help her find Amal. Where the hell was she? What was Amal up to?

Sitting in the rental car in the hot sun was not going to help her find her best friend. As she stepped out of the car, her cell phone tumbled from her pocket and landed on the floorboard. Reaching down to grab it, she noticed a small corner of smooth red fabric extending from underneath the seat. Tugging at it, more of the fabric was revealed. A red silk scarf. The same silk red scarf Vivian had loaned to Amal to wear to the street circus.

Vivian pulled harder. The scarf seemed stuck under the seat. Reaching her hand underneath, she felt a hard, smooth object, wrapped in the silky textile. Dislodging it, Vivian stood and unraveled the object from the folds of the fabric. Waves of confusion and dread washed over her as she stared at the large black gun gleaming in the sunlight.

Chapter Fourteen

"Why does Detective François want to talk to me?" Vivian asked the officer, a laconic, bleary-eyed man with a lazy St. Killian drawl.

The deputy shook his head. "No idea. Just wants you to wait here for him."

Moments ago, Vivian had gone through with her plans to file a missing person report for Amal. She wasn't completely convinced the missing person report was necessary, but after finding the gun in the abandoned car Amal had rented, Vivian had been compelled to get the police involved.

Going off the grid during a vacation was something Amal had done before, but Vivian feared Amal's latest disappearing act was different. Her best friend might really be in trouble.

Restless, Vivian searched for a clock in the sterile conference room where she'd been instructed to wait. On a table in the corner, a small microwave sat next to a coffee maker. The digital time display read 4:52 p.m.

Vivian exhaled, shifting in the uncomfortable folding chair. With three stories to file for tomorrow's edition, she didn't have time to talk to the detective. Nevertheless, one of the articles needed a quote from the St. Killian Police Department, which Vivian had requested a few days ago but hadn't received. Maybe Baxter had decided to give her an official statement.

While she had his attention, Vivian planned to convince him to search for Amal. Despite the missing person report, the cops probably wouldn't even think Amal was missing and would assume Vivian was overreacting.

A missing tourist was bad for business. No one wanted to visit an island where they might be abducted. The police, on behalf of the minister of tourism, would treat a missing person as someone who probably got caught up in an island fling and forgot to call and check in.

Vivian had to make sure Baxter François took her seriously. She couldn't allow the lawman to dismiss her concerns about Amal. And she had to be careful about what she told the detective. She wouldn't lie to Baxter François, but she wasn't going to give him all the facts either. She would tell him she hadn't heard from Amal in two days and about the abandoned rental car, but she wouldn't mention anything about the gun.

She wanted the detective to focus on looking for Amal, not on why Amal had illegally purchased a nine-millimeter Glock—something Vivian wanted to know herself and planned to find out once Amal was found.

Vivian shivered, thinking about the large, black pistol she'd found beneath the driver's seat of the car Amal had rented, and then abandoned, for whatever reason. Instinctively, Vivian had taken the gun and the red scarf and hidden them in the glove box of her Range Rover. Maybe not the best move, but she didn't want Amal to get into trouble for possessing an illegal firearm. Of course, now *she* was in possession of the illegal firearm, Vivian realized, shaking her head, wishing she hadn't been so hasty about the gun.

Fifteen minutes later, the door to the small conference room opened. Vivian sat up, her body straight and rigid and her heart pounding, as a tall, handsome, well-built man stepped into the room, carrying a manila file and a steno pad. Well-dressed in a blazer, polo shirt, and tailored slacks, he gave her a polite nod and closed the door behind him.

"Good afternoon, Ms. Thomas," he said, taking the seat at the head of the conference table. "It's nice to see you again. Sorry you had to wait so long, but I had to take a call at the last minute."

"No problem," Vivian said. "Actually, I need to talk to you."

"Is that right?" The detective gave her a slight smile.

"You're probably not aware of this," Vivian began, "but I came to the police station to file a missing person report, and—"

"One of the deputies did inform me about that," said the detective, looking down at his steno pad, opened to a page littered with chicken scratch. "The report was for a woman named Amal Shahin, correct?"

"Yes, that's correct."

"And how do you know Ms. Shahin?"

"She's my best friend."

The detective made a steeple of his fingers as he glanced at the ceiling. "And, in your missing person report, you said that the last time you saw or spoke to Ms. Shahin was two days ago, correct?"

"Right," answered Vivian, feeling as though the detective had turned the tables on her. She'd intended to influence and interview him, but now he was interrogating her. "I'm worried about her, and I would like the police to take my concerns seriously and make a sincere effort to find my friend."

The detective gave her a patient smile, but Vivian caught the flash of concern in his dark eyes. Exhaling, the detective asked, "You believe that something bad has happened to Ms. Shahin?"

"That's why I filed the missing person report."

"I'm curious about something," said the detective. "Ms. Shahin is your best friend, and you think something bad may have happened to her, and yet you waited two days to file the missing person report? Why is that?"

Vivian cleared her throat. "Detective François, I'm not sure how to explain it, but I wasn't worried about Amal until now because she's done this before and—"

"She's done what before?" the detective asked. "Gone missing?"

"What I mean is," Vivian said, hoping she wouldn't make things worse, "when we've gone on vacation before, Amal has often gone on excursions without telling me. But, she's never been gone this long without contacting me. As I said, I think something bad may have happened to her, and I would appreciate it if you put forth as much effort as possible to find her."

"Ms. Thomas, I'm afraid I can't do that." The detective let out a long exhale, rubbing the hint of stubble on his jaw.

"Why not?" Vivian asked, indignant. "Are you worried about how bad publicity might affect the tourism industry? If that's the case, then I can make sure the story about Amal's disappearance isn't published in the paper."

"Ms. Thomas, I'm not worried about bad publicity," he said. "Right now, I'm more worried about how you're going to be affected by what I have to tell you."

Vivian's stomach dropped. "What are you talking about?"

"I have some bad news."

Vivian stared at the detective, her heart pounding. "What kind of bad news?"

The detective cleared his throat. "One of your colleagues wrote a story about a hit-and-run victim found in the parking lot of a local bar."

Curious and yet wary, Vivian nodded. "Right. Beanie—Roland Bean—wrote that piece, I think. Why are you bringing up that story? Does the police department have a problem with Beanie's article? Did he misquote a detective or something? Is the bad news that the department is suing the *Palmchat Gazette*?"

"Mr. Bean did a decent job with the story, considering that he didn't have all the facts," the detective said.

"What facts didn't he have?" Vivian asked, anxious to know the bad news and yet fearing what it might be. "I seem to recall something about an eyewitness?"

"That's right," the detective said. "A local farmer—Jesse Chambray—witnessed the accident and saw the driver fleeing the scene in a late-model orange Toyota Corolla. Mr. Chambray didn't get the license plates. He was too shaken up by what he'd seen, and of course, he wanted to help the victim."

"So, I'm guessing you haven't found the driver of the orange Toyota?" Vivian asked, though she knew the answer to her question and felt as though she was stalling, terrified of learning the bad news.

"No, but we're still looking," the detective confirmed. "My guess is that, like most hit-and-run cases, the driver panicked and left instead of stopping to render aid."

"Well, I don't think Beanie knew the name of the eyewitness," Vivian said and dug in her purse for her cell phone. "Maybe he can interview Mr. Chambray. And maybe you can give me a statement for Beanie."

"Vivian …"

She gasped, jolted by the deep resonance of his voice, and stared at him, her heart slamming, fearful of the sympathy in his dark eyes.

"The hit-and-run victim was found with a purse," he said.

"A purse?" Vivian felt heat marching up her neck, like angry fire ants. "It was a woman?"

"There was a wallet in the purse," the detective continued. "We found the victim's identification."

"You know who she was?"

The detective nodded, solemn. "I wish I didn't have to tell you this …"

"Tell me what?"

Grim, the detective said, "The hit-and-run victim was your friend … Amal Shahin."

Chapter Fifteen

Vivian's eyes followed the ceiling fan, turning round and round.

She'd collapsed on her king-sized bed, after returning to the condo following the surreal encounter at the police station. It had been seventeen hours since Vivian learned of her best friend's death. Seventeen hours watching the ceiling fan, sleep eluding her as her body shut down. Unwilling to accept that Amal was gone, she was unable to feel anything from the unexpected loss.

"Would you like to see the body?"

Detective Baxter François' words from yesterday trespassed into her mind. He'd nudged her toward the gruesome option, perhaps because she'd had no reaction to his words. No tears. No sadness. No acknowledgment.

She'd taken that option, hoping to disprove the detective's claims about Amal being the hit-and-run victim from the Purple Gecko parking lot. Gazing in disbelief at Amal's body, Vivian thought she looked so beautiful. The beauty was marred by purple blotches on Amal's skin. The bruises, cuts, and scrapes were remnants of the tragic way she'd died.

Vivian had brushed her hand along Amal's face and was jolted by the coldness of her pallid skin. Jerking her hand away, she'd turned and run out of the room, her heart seizing in her chest as she gasped for breath.

The ceiling fan continued to turn, lulling Vivian into a catatonic state as memories assaulted her. Images of Amal under the harsh bright lights of the morgue, lying lifelessly on the metal table jumbled with the detective's words announcing her death. She'd been unable to make sense of it all, reverting to her reporter's instincts.

"Baxter, I don't think this was an accident."

"Why do you say that?" A hint of pity flashed across the detective's eyes before he led her back to the conference room.

"Amal bought a gun." The words rushed from her, an avalanche of everything she'd found out before arriving at the police station to file the missing person report. "Landon George helped her, and she rented a car to go to the Purple Gecko. You know he's a criminal. What if she got caught in one of his crimes and was run over on purpose?"

"How do you know all of this?" Raising an eyebrow, the detective scribbled on the steno pad.

"Landon told me, and I found the gun under the seat in the car Amal rented."

Vivian had led one of the deputies out to her Range Rover to retrieve the gun. She gave them a copy of the rental car agreement and told them in detail, for the second time, what Landon had said about his encounter with Amal. Detective François had promised to look into everything she'd shared.

Vivian didn't remember driving back to her condo that night or walking into her master bedroom, collapsing onto the bed before burrowing herself under the covers. Her lack of reaction to Amal's death was a result of years of practice dealing with daily atrocities.

As a reporter in some of the most war-ravaged hellholes in the world, Vivian had seen suffering and diabolical torture. She'd seen heartbreaking deaths and dead bodies before. Despite the horror she witnessed, she'd managed to compartmentalize the losses, needing to be immune to provide fair and balanced reports without the bias of her feelings, perceptions, and judgments. Her job was to gather facts and disseminate them in a concise manner. She wasn't to editorialize or allow the dire circumstances to wreck her emotions and thus steal her objectivity.

This time the death was Amal's.

There should've been no inoculation against the death of a woman who had been more than a friend, more like a sister, a refuge, an anchor. Amal had been her closest confidant. When her five-year fairy-tale romance with Leo ended abruptly, Vivian flew into a tailspin of regrettable behavior. As Vivian thawed from the pain, Amal was the only person she'd wanted to talk to, the only one she trusted with the truth. Welcoming her back to the land of the living, Amal had been selfless enough just to listen as Vivian had cried, pouring out her heart. She'd been supportive without judgment, without chiding Vivian for throwing her life away over a man. Amal had been the only one who understood, pulling Vivian slowly out of her misery with comfort and a bit of tough love.

That had been the lowest time of her life until yesterday. Seeing Amal's cold, still body, a relic of the vibrant and vivid woman she'd been, was more than Vivian could bear.

Chapter Sixteen

An invisible barrier of mourning had settled on the small courtyard as Vivian sat at the bistro table. Staring at the sundrenched hibiscus flowers in full bloom, she rubbed her temples and leaned her elbows on her knees. The phone call with Amal's parents had ended almost thirty minutes ago, and she was still numb. Amal's mother had been distraught, unable to speak through muffled cries. Her father was more stoical, reciting the details of Amal's funeral next week in Cairo. Amal had been their only child, the center of their world, and now she was gone.

Vivian had spared them the truth of Amal's trip to St. Killian. A truth she was still trying to uncover. Over the past three days, Vivian had poured through every detail of Amal's last day alive. Thinking back on that day, Vivian had known Amal was distracted and annoyed by something. The incessant texts at lunch had irritated her best friend. Amal had claimed everything was fine, so Vivian hadn't pushed her for more.

Vivian took a deep breath and held it for several seconds before releasing it slowly. Looking down at her hands, she released her clenched fingers, wiggling them until the ache began to subside. A nagging thought had infected her at the police station after viewing Amal's body. The more she recounted Amal's unusual behavior, the more it took root.

Amal's death was not an accident.

Amal had lied about her interest in Landon. The sexy waiter was a fence to get her a gun illegally. Why had Amal bought a gun as soon as she arrived in St. Killian? Had Amal known there was some threat waiting for her on the island?

It didn't make sense. If there had been a threat to Amal's life in St. Killian, why had she come here? Amal could have stayed safe in Palm Beach or planned this trip to some other island. Vivian wouldn't have protested.

"I want to raise a glass to myself because no one is ever going to make a fool of me again."

Vivian shuddered.

She'd forgotten about Amal's statement in their raise a glass game, until now. Could that one remark be the key to discovering the truth? Vivian thought about her tenacious friend. Amal had never scared easily, and she couldn't imagine her cowering to any threat. She was tough. The type to confront and not hide. Amal had made it a priority to get a gun while she was here. Was it for protection or had there been a different motive? One that had gone terribly wrong and had ended her life?

Grabbing her cell phone, Vivian scrolled through the contacts listing until she found the number she was looking for and pressed the talk button.

"Phoenix Wellness and Spa," said a lyrical, soft-spoken female voice. "This is Snowdrop. How may I help you?"

"Hi, um ... Snowdrop," Vivian said, unsure of whether Amal's employees at the medical spa had been told about her death. "This is Vivian Thomas. I'm Ms. Shahin's best friend."

"Hi, Ms. Thomas. Ms. Shahin told me she was vacationing with you."

From the woman's calm demeanor, Vivian knew she was

unaware of the hit-and-run accident that had killed her boss. Pausing, Vivian contemplated whether she should deliver the news or allow Amal's parents to do it. Withholding the information from the assistant was cruel, but this could be Vivian's only chance to get what she desired from Snowdrop—information about the vendor Amal had threatened to kill. Amal downplayed the incident, claiming it was a problem with her purchase of massage tables. Vivian hadn't believed Amal's explanation, but again she hadn't pressed for more details. Could the dispute with the vendor have led to Amal's death?

"Has Amal contacted you?" Vivian asked, choosing to take advantage of the limited opportunity. "You know, to check in and see how things are going?"

"Not at all. Ms. Shahin said she needed to relax and spend quality time with her best friend. I haven't talked to her since before she flew out to St. Killian."

Vivian hesitated, surprised and confused by Snowdrop's answer.

"Has she been trying to reach me?" Snowdrop asked, concern seeping in her tone. "Do you think I should call her? I don't want to bother her because I know she needs to relax, but maybe she would want to know about the private investigator."

"Private investigator?"

"This P.I. from Dallas has been calling nonstop," Snowdrop said, a trace of annoyance in her tone. "He says she won't answer her cell. I tried to explain to him that Ms. Shahin is on vacation. She probably turned her phone off, but he keeps calling. I think he's worried about her, but I don't know why. She's on a beautiful, tropical island with her best friend. He doesn't need to worry."

"What's the private investigator's name?"

"One sec." Snowdrop paused. The sound of papers rustling in the background filtered through the phone. "I have it right here. Jake Frankowski."

"You have his number?"

Snowdrop rattled off ten digits and then said, "I have another call coming in. Can I put you on hold?"

"No, actually, I'll let you go." Repeating the ten digits in her mind, Vivian rose from the bistro table and headed through the garage and back into her condo. Grabbing a pen from a cabinet drawer, she scrawled the name and number of the P.I. onto a sticky note from the dispenser next to the cordless kitchen phone. Staring at the words she'd just written, Vivian tapped the pen against the paper as an uneasiness settled within her.

More lies from Amal. Whatever texts and phone calls she was making on her first and only day alive in St. Killian were not to her assistant as she'd said. Who had Amal been talking to when Vivian overheard her threatening to kill someone? And who had she wanted to kill?

What was the deal with the private investigator? Why had he been trying to reach Amal? Why would he be worried about Amal?

Grabbing the cordless phone, Vivian dialed the private investigator's phone number determined to find out why he needed to talk to Amal. After three rings, the phone was answered.

"Frankowski Investigations, can I help you?" Another female voice, but this one sounded irritated and raspy.

"Jake Frankowski, please."

"He's out to lunch," the woman said. "You wanna leave a message?"

"Um, no, I'll call back."

Vivian cursed. Of course, he would be at lunch when she was desperate to talk to him.

A knock on the door startled Vivian from her thoughts. Laying the phone on the counter, she walked through the living room to her front door and looked through the peephole.

Detective François stood on the other side, smartly dressed in a plaid shirt and dark blue trousers. Vivian glanced down at the dingy sweatshirt and cotton pajama bottoms she'd spent the last three days in and shrugged. She had no time to worry about her appearance. The detective could have vital information about Amal's death.

Opening the door wide, Vivian stared at him. Baxter François' eyes narrowed as he took in her haggard appearance. Vivian turned and walked into the living room, sitting on the couch. Following her inside, Baxter closed the door behind him and remained standing.

"How are you doing?" he asked softly, after a short pause.

Vivian waved a hand dismissively in response.

"I stopped by the paper to see you. Mr. Bean said you were taking a couple of weeks off. I think that's a good idea."

"I didn't know detectives made house calls. Are you here just to check up on me or do you have any news about Amal's death?"

"Both. I know we've only interacted in a ... professional capacity, but I'd like to think that along the way we've forged a friendship of sorts." Baxter walked over to the couch and sat next to her. "This is a difficult time for you, and what I have to tell you is not going to make it any easier."

Vivian's heart began to pound. "What is it?"

"I brought Landon in for questioning. He denied taking your friend to purchase a gun. He said he was just being friendly, driving a tourist back to her friend's condo because she'd grown tired of the street circus." Baxter clasped his hands and leaned forward, glancing at Vivian before continuing. "Vivian, he has an alibi for the time of Amal's death. Over two hundred witnesses at Club Chivo danced as he deejayed from ten that night until five the next morning."

Vivian felt her body began to deflate. "And the gun?"

"No fingerprints on it but yours. There's no proof Amal bought the gun, and there's no crime in renting a car to try out a local bar, even if it is one in a less than desirable part of the island."

Vivian's body was heavy with disappointment.

"Vivian, look at me," the detective implored.

Turning toward him, Vivian saw the concern and compassion in his dark brown eyes.

"This was a senseless accident. Your friend was just in the wrong place at the wrong time."

The detective reached over to grab her hand in slow motion as a tsunami of grief crashed over her. The torrent of tears began to flow, shaking Vivian's body uncontrollably with each sob. At that moment, Vivian wasn't sure she'd ever stop crying.

Chapter Seventeen

Rushing into the oversized foyer of Burt Bronson's mansion, located in the exclusive neighborhood of Marchmont on the northern coast, Vivian hurried over to the petite nurse, pacing in front of the spiral staircase. An hour ago, she'd received an urgent text.

Burt needs you. It's an emergency. Come over right away.

Seven months prior, Burt had suffered a massive heart attack while on the golf course. Not willing to be confined to a hospital bed, he demanded to be released early and blazed through a six-week rehabilitation program in three weeks to get back to work at the newspaper. He'd bragged about his quick recovery, but it was short-lived.

"Dixie, what happened with Burt?" Vivian asked, trying not to panic.

"Oh, Ms. Vivian, he's been on one of his tirades," Nurse Dixie said, shaking her head. "I know I'm getting on his nerves right now, but he's so stubborn and hardheaded. He won't follow my instructions and rest. He insists on working! He's up there right now, as we speak, doing entirely too much. Then he yells at me for trying to get him to stop. You're the only one who can get through to him, so please, convince him to rest."

Relieved and slightly annoyed by the nurse's false alarm, Vivian gave her a gentle squeeze.

"I'll do my best," Vivian said, heading upstairs to the master bedroom suite. Shortly after Vivian had returned from Amal's funeral in Cairo, she'd plunged into work as a distraction, and Burt had mimicked her actions, hiding from his medical issues. They'd been working late editing her article on the local mayor's race when Burt suddenly slumped over and slid out of his dark leather chair onto the floor in a heap.

Vivian had rushed to check his pulse. It was weak, but Burt was still breathing. She'd called an ambulance and then sat on the floor cradling the man who'd become her mentor over the past year, fearful of another loss of someone important to her. The ride to the hospital was tense, and Vivian berated herself for allowing Burt to work late. She knew he was still recovering from his heart attack. Why hadn't she forced him to go home and rest?

Later at the hospital, she'd found out that this was the third time he'd been rushed to the emergency room for a blackout in as many weeks. The diagnosis of his fainting spells had been devastating—severe heart failure and a sentence of six months of bed rest under nurse supervision until his heart stabilized.

Confined in his home for the past month, Burt had become more difficult. He was in denial and suffered from bouts of rage and anxiety. Paranoia about the newspaper failing without him at the helm had distressed him. For a while, he'd been content with performing the editorial duties from his bed. But most days he battled severe exhaustion, sleeping for fifteen hours with no energy to critique the articles before they were published.

Vivian peered through the bedroom door at Burt. His face was pained, and his robust body looked worn and deflated. It was still shocking to see her boss weak and downtrodden.

Hearing another man's voice wafting from the room, Vivian

paused at the top of the stairs, straining to hear the conversation. Nurse Dixie had mentioned Burt was working, but she didn't say he was working with someone. A sudden wave of warmth flushed her skin as she recognized the male voice.

Leo.

Over a month had passed since they'd made love on the beach during the street circus. That moment felt like a lifetime ago. Vivian never thought she would see him again. Her best friend Amal had died that same night, and the loss was a wake-up call for Vivian.

Life was too precious for her to waste another moment pining after a man who was unwilling to give her the life she deserved. Forcing herself to accept Leo's stance on marriage had been diffi-cult, but Vivian squelched the last flame of hope she'd had for rekindling their relationship. What they'd shared would always be an important chapter in her life, but she no longer fantasized about a reunion that would never happen. She had started to date again, and even though she had no serious prospects, she was enjoying getting to know other men and exploring the possibilities of finding love again.

But now that Leo was less than twenty feet away from her, a soft flutter danced in her stomach, a hint of joy blossoming from the thought of seeing him again. Vivian had thought she was finally over Leo. Why the hell was she feeling tingly all over? When would she ever get past these feelings?

Vivian wanted to scream. There had always been a chance Leo would show up to visit his father. She'd convinced herself that his presence wouldn't affect her. Yet, here he was, and she was actually excited about the chance to see him again. Even if it was just a glimpse.

A part of her would always cherish what she'd shared with Leo, but nothing had changed between them. She couldn't allow herself to hope for something out of reach. Her mind knew it was pointless to keep wanting Leo. She needed her heart to get to that same conclusion.

Vivian flattened her body against the wall where she'd be unseen by Burt and Leo. Why was Leo here? Maybe Burt's relapse was an admonition, finally compelling him to confide in his son about his medical condition. She'd detected a change in Burt since his last episode, a recognition of his mortality and an increased willingness to accept help. After his first heart attack, the *Palmchat Gazette* staff had been sworn to secrecy. He hadn't wanted to worry his son or his ex-wife and was convinced he'd be back to normal soon. This time was different. Burt's diagnosis was serious, and he needed more than a nurse's care to help him recover this time.

Through the open bedroom door, Vivian could see through Burt's window. Focusing on the perfect view of the island's most famous landmark, St. Killian's version of Cristo Redentor, perched on a small hill, Vivian tried to discern what the conversation was about. She caught certain phrases, enough to realize Leo was arguing with Burt about the newspaper. Raising his voice, agitated but persistent, Burt said something about doing things his way. Leo wasn't backing down. His responses were loud but calm and decisive. There was a casual professionalism in the delivery, the natural confidence Leo had always exuded. Burt had more than met his match. Leo was winning the argument and not just because Burt was exhausted and confined to bed rest.

Vivian took a few steps back down the stairs and contemplated her next move. There was no reason to insert herself in their father-son drama. Whatever their disagreements, it was up to the two of them to resolve. Burt was perturbed but obviously not in any danger.

As she hesitated for a moment, Vivian knew seeing Leo again was too much to bear right now. Abandoning her dreams of a reunion with him was tenuous at best. She couldn't handle seeing him again without taking a huge step back in the progress she'd made. Turning to walk back down the spiral staircase, Vivian made a mental note to call Burt later.

As she reached the bottom step, she heard Leo's voice again, louder and more insistent.

"Viv? Is that you?"

Chapter Eighteen

Vivian froze, remaining silent. Her heart pounded in recognition of Leo's presence, yearning to see him in spite of her fears.

"What are you doing here?" Leo asked.

Vivian heard Leo's steps on the hardwood stairs growing louder as he came closer to her, sending flurries through her body. Turning slowly, she saw Leo beaming at her.

"Umm …" Vivian started, her mouth suddenly dry. "Dixie asked me to stop by and check on Burt. What are you doing here?"

"Playing the role of the dutiful son." Leo smirked as he crossed his arms over his muscular chest. "Old man's a damn fool, hiding these heart attacks from me for so long."

"He didn't want to worry you," Vivian said, unsure of what to do next.

Allowing herself a moment to enjoy the view, Vivian watched as Leo closed the distance between them. He was the epitome of understated allure, ruggedly handsome with a square jaw, scruffy beard, and a mane of unruly chestnut-brown hair giving him an unplanned GQ look. His muscular physique was barely contained in a casual light-blue cotton button-down shirt, his sleeves rolled to his elbows, and light-khaki pants. He could easily have been walking off the set of a modeling shoot.

Her weakness had always been his crystal light-blue eyes, bright and piercing, which had mesmerized her and captured her heart. With those eyes, he'd seen into her soul.

Leo stopped in front of her, a mere three feet separating them. His eyes roamed over her face as if memorizing every angle and curve.

"Well, since everything appears to be fine here and you're taking care of Burt, I'm going to head home." Vivian turned to walk back toward the oversized oak double doors, etched with biblical scenes in relief.

"Viv, wait." Leo touched her hand, stopping her. The fire she thought she'd quelled was still smoldering, ready to ignite once more. Turning her to face him, Leo caressed her shoulders, sparking warmth on her skin under the tenderness of his touch. She looked up into his eyes and felt the familiar longing and love.

"Burt told me about Amal. I'm so sorry."

Before Vivian could respond, Leo pulled her into a tight embrace. The feel of his body next to hers sent a rush of adrenaline through her. Melting into him, she felt weightless and free, comforted by the protective arms that had been her only solace for five years, living through cruelty in war-ravaged African countries. She'd wrestled with grief for weeks after Amal's death, managing her sorrow alone for the first time with no one to lean on. She'd yearned for this comfort from Leo during those weeks when thoughts of Amal lying lifeless within the police station haunted her nights. Vivian stiffened, unwilling to unleash the memories of the day she'd learned her best friend was the victim of a hit-and-run accident. Blinking back tears, she pulled away from Leo.

"Thank you," Vivian mumbled.

"Why didn't you ..." Leo started and then stopped, looking away for a moment, his jaw muscles clenching, before looking back at her. "I can't imagine how difficult it was to go through that ...

alone. If you need anything, anything at all, please call me. There's nothing I wouldn't do for you."

A flash of anger blinded Vivian, and she inhaled sharply. There was one important thing Leo had made it very clear he wouldn't do for her. How could he stand here in front of her and make a statement like that, knowing their history? Deciding not to bring up their past when Leo was trying to be supportive, Vivian just nodded. She didn't trust herself to speak, afraid of the venom she might spew on him.

"I think Burt would love to see you," Leo said, rubbing his hands along her arms. "My gut says he forced Dixie to ask you to come over. He's always had a soft spot for you. Why don't you go on up? I need to go take care of some things anyway."

"Yes, I'll do that," Vivian responded and headed back toward the staircase.

"Viv."

"Yes, Leo."

"It's really good to see you again."

Vivian smiled and then hurled herself up the stairs toward Burt's master bedroom before she did something she regretted.

Chapter Nineteen

Stopping outside Burt's bedroom door, Vivian squeezed her eyes shut, forcing the tears to recede. In one moment, Leo had catapulted her through a gauntlet of emotions from love to bitterness, sadness to anger. Leo overwhelmed her, and she was exhausted from fighting the battle to keep the emotions tempered. After several minutes of deep breathing, she pushed Leo into the recesses of her mind and focused on Burt.

Walking toward the bedroom, Vivian paused. He looked so much older, visibly traumatized by his condition, which was most likely exacerbated because of his argument with Leo.

"Hey," Vivian said softly, lightly knocking on the door before entering.

Burt looked up at her, exhaled heavily, and then waved his arm for her to come closer to his bed. Taking up her normal spot, she pulled the tufted cowhide chair from the corner, placed it next to the bed, and sat down.

Reaching over to hold one of Burt's hands, Vivian asked, "You okay? I heard you arguing with Leo."

"I'm fine. Now that you are here," Burt replied, his features relaxed. The grimace she'd seen earlier had faded.

"You don't look fine, Burt. You look harassed."

Burt let out a hearty laugh, and for one moment, she got a glimpse of the vibrant man he was several years ago when they first met. The first holidays she and Leo ever spent together, they'd flown to his high-rise condo in Vancouver for Christmas and spent four lively days being entertained by Burt and his cast of eclectic literary-centric friends.

"Despite my physical condition, that little tiff is not enough to wear me down. How are you, my dear?" Burt asked.

"Well, I'm a bit confused. Why did Dixie text me saying it was an emergency? You're fine, Burt."

"I needed to see you," Burt said. He was avoiding eye contact, his hands fidgeting with the edge of his robe.

"Why?"

"You should know why, now." Burt picked at the fringes of his robe and then looked Vivian squarely in the eyes. "I wanted to tell you about Leo before you saw him ... at work tomorrow."

"At work? At the *Palmchat Gazette*?" Nausea rose within Vivian at the thought of working side by side with Leo again. Was this a nightmare or her dream come true?

"He is the new interim editor-in-chief of the *Palmchat Gazette*." Burt squeezed her hand and then leaned back onto the mountain of pillows on his bed.

"Interim editor-in-chief," Vivian repeated, raising an eyebrow. She couldn't fathom how he'd convinced Leo to leave *The New York Times* to work for him. She released Burt's hand and leaned back in the chair, selfishly contemplating how she was going to manage to report to the man she was reluctant to admit she still loved.

Vivian was glad Burt was taking a full step away from all of his responsibilities at the paper. If he kept pushing himself, his heart would never recover, and he might need a transplant. She just wished he had chosen someone else, anyone else except Leo to take on the interim role.

"I hope you're not upset. I know this won't be easy for you, Vivian." Burt's words were genuine but gave Vivian no comfort.

"I've learned a lot about you over the past month," Burt continued, pointing a finger toward her. "You're tough and strong, and I know you can handle this. Plus, it's just temporary. Leo took a sabbatical from *The New York Times*. When I'm cleared in a few months, he plans to go back on assignment in Africa."

Burt gave her a weak smile.

"I'm not upset." Vivian lied, as she fought the urge to have a temper tantrum in the middle of Burt's bedroom. How could he have put her in this position? Why hadn't she left St. Killian a long time ago like Amal wanted her to? If she had, she wouldn't be in this predicament. She could just hear Amal chiding her right now.

I know your feelings for him haven't changed. You still love him. You still want to be with him. That's why you're terrified of seeing him again.

Putting her selfishness aside, Vivian said, "This is a good move for you. I'm glad you are starting to take your recovery seriously. The paper is in excellent hands. Leo is an amazing journalist, and you won't have to worry about work anymore."

"What did we Bronson men do to deserve such an amazing woman like you in our lives?"

"It's no big deal, really," Vivian said, more to reassure herself than Burt. "I won't lie, Burt, it's going to be awkward. We'll work through it though."

"But, it is a big deal," Burt insisted, his face flushed red with emotion, tears pooling in the corners of his eyes.

"Why do you say that?" Vivian asked, confused by the distress Burt displayed.

"Because I'm the reason Leo broke your heart."

Chapter Twenty

After unlocking the front door of her condo, Vivian waved to Sophie Carter, a rookie reporter at the *Palmchat Gazette,* who sat in an idling convertible Mercedes, waiting for Vivian to get inside safely.

They called out goodnights and proclamations of the fun they'd had, and then Vivian entered the condo, closing and locking the door behind her. Half-stumbling through the living room, she removed her left stiletto and then her right one as she headed to her bedroom.

Sophie and her sister Sinnamon, a hotel manager, had invited her to join them for a salacious Sunday afternoon. Vivian had resisted the urge to decline, thinking libations and lust might take her mind away from the sadness of Amal's death—and the confusion and frustration she couldn't shake following her encounter with Leo. Seeing him again had left her frazzled, but she had to get it together. He was back in her life, whether she liked it or not, and she had to be ready for him and the way her emotions went to war every time he was around.

Not willing to spend her evening ruminating over everything she regretted about the demise of their relationship, Vivian had instead gotten all glammed up and was ready to party when Sophie picked her up.

It was a little after three in the morning, and Vivian was drunk and exhausted.

The evening had started with happy hour at Breezy Daze, a chic dive packed to the gills with tourists and locals. From Breezy Daze, they moved on to an early dinner at Goat-A-Rama, and then they'd hightailed it to the marina to board the USS Shake Yo Booty for St. Killian's most popular booze cruise, dubbed Midnight Madness, known for being rowdy, raucous, and raunchy. Two hours of sexy, sweaty bodies swaying to reggae, salsa, samba, and even a bit of zydeco and nonstop shots, including the mysterious Sex on a Yacht, which, for a moment, had made Vivian feel as though she'd swallowed novocaine.

After stripping off her clothes in the bathroom, Vivian took a quick, hot shower and then climbed beneath the cool, smooth sheets.

Lying in bed, Vivian tossed and turned. She was exhausted but couldn't sleep. Each time she closed her eyes, she pictured Burt and heard the bomb he'd dropped reverberated in her mind like a mortar shell.

"It's my fault Leo broke your heart."

Eyes opened, abandoning her attempts to sleep, Vivian stared at the ceiling, remembering Burt's words.

Leo was a child of divorce, like so many other people. Like herself. Her parents had split up when she was three. Neither had remarried, but their life choices hadn't influenced her opinions about marriage. Despite spending the school year with her dad and summers with her mother, Vivian considered her childhood to have been happy, well-balanced, and normal. Had it been perfect? Of course not. But, neither had it been tortuous or contentious.

Her parents had realized, fairly quickly, they didn't belong together and weren't soul mates. Still, they were friends who liked and respected each other. More than anything, they were devoted to Vivian, dedicated to bringing her up in a loving, nurturing environment—even if one environment was frosty Alaska, where her father was the lead geologist at a major oil company, and the other was luxurious, exclusive Monaco, the base for her mother's international interior design company.

Although she had no memories of her parents as a married couple, Vivian had never allowed the lack of a marital role model to derail her hopes and dreams for a husband of her own. She'd never been afraid that her parent's divorce would taint, or curse, her marriage attempts. Her parents had divorced because while they admired each other, they were self-aware enough to realize their union lacked several critical hallmarks of a successful marriage—passion and love. There couldn't be dedication and devotion but no desire.

She and Leo weren't like her parents. They weren't colleagues who sometimes slept together because they were bored. She and Leo had been friends and lovers. It was all about love and passion between them which was why Vivian couldn't understand Leo's aversion to making the relationship official.

Well, she supposed she knew now. Burt had certainly opened her eyes, but Vivian didn't like the vision before her.

Vivian rolled over onto her side and stared at the moonlit palms swaying in the breeze outside her window.

Burt and Leo's mother, Aurora Nathaniel, the billionaire heiress of Au'Naturale Cosmetics, had been instant lovers. Blessed with a fairy-tale love story—eyes meeting across the room, an immediate connection, and an undeniable need to be with each other—they had moved in together a week after meeting at a fundraising gala in Manhattan.

Three years later, still blissfully in love, Burt and Aurora had conceived Leo while on a trip to Tanzania.

Fifteen years later, when Leo was a smart, gregarious, rambunctious twelve-year-old who played soccer, football, and the tuba, Burt and Aurora decided to make things official between them.

With Leo serving as their best man, Burt and Aurora tied the knot before five hundred guests in Paris, at the Palace of Versailles, on a beautiful, crisp, sunny day. After honeymooning on a private island in the Indian Ocean, the newlyweds returned to New York, eager to begin domestic bliss, and all their family and friends believed they would be victorious.

All their family and friends had been horribly wrong.

Moving onto her stomach, Vivian pressed her face against the cool pillow and then crossed and uncrossed her ankles.

A year after their magical fairy-tale wedding in France, their amazing love had turned to disgust, distrust, and despair. Leo had witnessed the decimation of his parents' relationship. Worse, the impressionable thirteen-year-old had heard Burt and Aurora spewing vitriolic opinions about the reason for the death of their love—marriage.

Burt had confessed that he'd told Leo never to get married, especially if things were going good. Marriage, Burt had promised Leo, would screw everything up. As a result, Leo grew up believing marriage was a curse, one which would rob him of true love. Leo was terrified of marriage, Burt had revealed, and thought the institution would lead to him hating the love of his life.

Vivian flopped over onto her back.

Leo had always been guarded about his childhood, and Vivian didn't recall many conversations with him about his parents. She couldn't remember if he'd told her they had split up when he was younger. Burt had said the acrimonious divorce had rendered Leo sullen, belligerent, and somewhat violent, instigating several schoolyard fights. Aurora and Burt had taken him to see a counselor, who specialized in treating children traumatized by divorce, but Leo never said a word during the sessions, despite coaxing from the therapist, and eventually, therapy was abandoned.

According to Burt, Leo never spoke of the divorce, and he never talked about one parent to the other. When he was with Aurora, it was as if he were a fatherless child. With Burt, he was motherless. Vivian didn't understand Leo's need to compartmentalize his parents, and could only deduce his behavior was some self-induced coping mechanism.

Vivian was saddened, knowing what Leo had suffered because of his parent's lack of concern and compassion for him. Burt's and Aurora's selfishness had been a form of abuse. Leo hadn't been afflicted with bruises and cuts, but he'd been crippled emotionally.

Now that Vivian had a better understanding of Leo's hostility toward marriage, she realized Burt had certainly been right. It was his fault that Leo hadn't wanted to marry her.

Closing her eyes again, Vivian reflected on Burt's reasons for Leo's presence on the island and at the paper.

After he finally learned about Burt's heart attack, Leo had been worried and upset, determined to do whatever it took to help his father. Burt had been thankful for Leo's willingness to take over the publishing responsibilities while he recovered. Burt knew Leo had a vastly different point of view concerning the editorial direction of the paper, but he thought the change might be good, might light a fire under the St. Killian reporters who'd become somewhat complacent.

Sighing, Vivian repositioned herself beneath the bed linens, seeking a position of comfort, one which would facilitate sleep as she remembered the favor Burt had requested from her, the favor she'd agreed to carry out.

Had she made Burt a promise she wouldn't be able to deliver?

Will you watch out for my son? Help him out? Show him the ropes at the paper, so he doesn't stumble too much.

Working in proximity with Leo was the last thing Vivian wanted to do despite her vow to Burt. Being around him day after day while she struggled to keep her feelings from getting out of control might be too difficult. And yet, she would be professional and polite.

As exhaustion finally caused her eyelids to droop, Vivian burrowed beneath the covers, thoughts whispering in her mind.

"You decided to stay in St. Killian to avoid dealing with what happened between you and Leo. We both know why you don't want to go back to Africa ... You're afraid to see Leo. You still love him. You still want to be with him. That's why you're terrified of seeing him again."

Jolted by the memory of Amal's words, so vivid and clear, Vivian sat up in bed, her heart pounding. Eyes sweeping the room, she peered at the shadowy corners, half-expecting her best friend to appear, half-wishing she would, as an angel in a red dress.

Vivian wished Leo could have somehow understood that his parents' horrendous relationship didn't mean he would fail at marriage. She wished he could realize he was wrong to think he would eventually hate her if they'd married. Even so, Vivian realized she had to give up the fantasies of being with Leo, making a life with him as man and wife. She couldn't waste time dwelling on the past or wishing for something she could never have. One day, maybe Leo would let go of his deep-seated, yet misguided, beliefs. Maybe the terrible ideology his parents had no business instilling in him would be overcome, but Vivian knew she wasn't going to be the woman to help him see the light. She couldn't. She had too much dignity and self-respect to chase after a man who was resolute in his opinions and unlikely to change his mind. Vivian still loved Leo, but the conversation with Burt reinforced her belief that she deserved a man who wanted the same things in life she did. Trying to change Leo was foolish and pointless. Despite Leo's feelings for her, Vivian suspected his staunch aversion to marriage would always keep him from making the commitment she wanted.

Lying back against the pillows, Vivian realized she couldn't stay stuck in the past, couldn't let failed hopes and dreams cause her to be bitter and resentful.

No more wishing, hoping and praying for things that weren't going to happen, no matter how much she'd wanted them to, Vivian told herself as her eyelids closed.

No more believing in fairy tales that never came true.

Chapter Twenty-One

Mutiny raged on the newsroom floor as Vivian walked through the glass doors of the *Palmchat Gazette*. A jumble of raised voices clamored over each other, desperate to have their opinions heard.

Rounding the corner into the newsroom—a large open space with reporters' desks lined along the perimeter of the walls—Vivian noticed Sophie Carter sitting silently, her face a mask of confused fury as she stared blankly at several pages of her story. The white 8 1/2-x-11 paper seemed to be bleeding from the red scribbles scrawled in the margins and between the sentences.

Walking past Sophie, Vivian approached three senior staff writers—Caleb Olivier, Stevie Bishop, and Roland "Beanie" Bean—clustered around a desk at the back of the room. Faces contorted in anger, each clutched their own pages smeared with comments in red.

Leo stood in the middle of the three men and absorbed the verbal assault with his arms crossed, showing off his biceps muscles. Although he was dressed in a casual and relaxed style, a plain V-neck white T-shirt and khaki cargo pants, he looked harassed, and his body was tense with frustration.

From the litany of complaints, Vivian figured the journalists wholeheartedly disagreed with his editorial comments on their respective stories. Burt was a tough editor, but he'd amended his feedback style to match the laid-back, reserved nature of the St. Killian people. Coming from *The New York Times*, Leo was used to a more direct approach, where sensitivity and feelings were checked at the door to ensure the best stories were published. He was ill-prepared to mollycoddle and babysit high-maintenance reporters whose feathers were easily ruffled. To make matters worse, she suspected the journalists were resentful because Burt hadn't asked one of them to take over his editorial duties while he convalesced.

Vivian massaged the back of her neck. She wasn't in the mood to break up a playground battle of hurt feelings on the newsroom floor right now. After tossing and turning all night, Vivian wanted nothing more than to curl up on the large, leather couch in Burt's office and nap. She had promised Burt she'd show Leo the ropes, though. Given the chaos she witnessed, obviously Leo was stumbling and needed help.

"Hey!" Vivian yelled, alerting the four men to her presence. "What is going on? Why are you screaming at each other?"

"I don't care where this boy came from and what fancy American newspaper he works at, I'm not a child! I'm a damn good journalist," Caleb vented. "I've been writing for my people for over twenty years, and he can't come in here and tell me that I'm doing it wrong."

"I haven't gotten this many comments on an article since I was writing for my high school newspaper, and I'm way better than that now," Stevie whined and looked earnestly at Vivian for some sign of approval.

"I'm not making any of these changes. If he don't like it, he can write all the articles himself, and I can go home and be with my wife and kids. I don't have time for this." Beanie huffed and walked back to his desk, leaning against it after slapping the pages onto the floor.

Vivian had to stifle a smile as she glanced at Leo. Rubbing his hands down the side of his face, he looked battered and confused, unprepared for the onslaught his comments had unleashed in the newsroom.

Vivian guessed Leo hoped to be the kind of editor he enjoyed working with—one with a sharp, critical eye who encouraged independence and provided constructive critique, which helped to hone and sharpen writing skills. The *Palmchat Gazette* staff, however, would need a bit of hand holding and effusive encouragement to complete assignments effectively, if not always efficiently.

"Help me," Leo mouthed to Vivian, his eyes pleading with her to fix the mess he'd made. She had to stifle a laugh and maintain a straight face if her plan was going to work.

"Caleb, Stevie, Beanie, we all know that Burt would expect for us to give his son," Vivian said, pausing for dramatic effect, "the same respect that you'd give him. But if you guys don't want to work with Burt's son, then I'll let him know."

The three men looked uncomfortable, most likely trying to weigh whether Vivian was bluffing or not.

"Wait now, there's no need to be hasty. I think we can be flexible and adjust to Mr. Leo's editorial style," Caleb said and looked over at Beanie and Stevie, both nodding their heads in agreement.

"I can make all my edits. I was just shocked by how many there were," Stevie said, as he rushed back over to his desk. "But, now that I look at them again, they really will make my story better. I can get these changes done in a few hours."

"Are you sure?" Vivian asked, knowing she had made her point.

The three Killian journalists confirmed and went back to work fixing their articles.

Vivian walked past Leo, indicating with a point of her index finger that he should follow her to the editor-in-chief's corner office. As Leo closed the door, Vivian headed to the comfy leather couch she coveted and stretched out across it.

"Thanks, Viv. Don't know what I would have done if you hadn't shown up when you did." Leo slumped down in the oversized chair behind the large mahogany desk. "Good to know we still make a great team."

There was a time when Vivian had thought she and Leo could tackle anything and be successful when they did it together, but she no longer believed in that fairy tale.

Unable to sleep last night, Vivian had decided to move on with her life. Committed to fulfilling the decisions she'd reached during her three a.m. epiphany, she was resigned to not waste any more time dwelling on the past. No more wishing for something she couldn't have. No matter how difficult it might be, she had to come to terms with the truth she had previously been too afraid to confront. Leo wasn't going to change. Despite her feelings for him, Vivian knew it was time to forget about happily ever after with Leo. Time to give up dreams that weren't going to come true, no matter how much she'd wanted them to.

"Sometimes we do," she conceded and then added, "other times we don't. Depends on what we're trying to accomplish if we have the same goals, the same motives."

"We're always good together, Viv," he said, deep voice lowered, thick with the memories of a decadent lust, with the promise of passion, hers for the taking, if she wanted it. And she did. Badly.

Vivian glanced at the water stains on the ceiling.

Passion came with a high price, though, one she'd paid before but now could no longer afford.

Trying to combat the effects of his presence, Vivian redirected the subject. "Unfortunately, Caleb, Stevie, and Beanie can be a bit sensitive. But, what you have to understand about them is that—"

"We can talk about that later," Leo interjected.

"But it's important that you know—"

"I was thinking about what happened to Amal," Leo said, piercing blue eyes full of tender compassion. "I hate that she was taken from you so randomly."

Tears threatened, but Vivian held them at bay. She didn't want to cry in front of Leo, even though she had so many times before when the travesties and atrocities of the Sudan got to be too much. Leo would hold her in his comforting embrace, leaving her free to unravel in his arms. But, after last night, she couldn't allow herself the luxury of his comfort.

"For what it's worth," Leo said, "I talked to a few of our sources at the St. Killian Police Department. They don't have any leads from the information the eyewitness gave them, but Detective François hasn't forgotten about the case, even though it's not one of his active investigations."

"Thanks." Vivian glanced at him and managed a shaky smile. Over the past month, she'd thought a lot about the circumstances surrounding Amal's death. Often, she'd thought of querying the detective for a progress report, but given his opinions of her speculations, Vivian didn't want his placating sympathy.

"I'm hoping they'll find out who killed her, so Amal can have justice," Leo said. "And you can have some peace, knowing the person who ended her life is behind bars."

Vivian felt a familiar tugging at her heart. Touched by his concern, she stared at the ceiling again. She wasn't surprised by his compassion. Leo had always been sympathetic, sensitive, and supportive, but she couldn't take his kindness to heart, couldn't allow it to change her mind about her decision to move on with her life without him.

"Listen, about Caleb, Stevie, and Beanie," Vivian tried again, wary of the moment between them becoming too poignant, worried she would lose her resolve to move on without him.

"Wasn't trying to be an asshole," Leo insisted, leaning forward and resting his elbows on the desk. "Just didn't realize I'd create so much commotion with the edits."

"It wasn't the edits. They're used to Burt asking for rewrites. It was the delivery." Leaving the couch, Vivian walked to the desk and sat on the edge, facing Leo. "They've never had their stories marked up like that. Burt usually discusses with them the changes he wants made. Actually, your father employs the same advice you gave me—you catch more flies with honey."

"I'm used to seasoned journalists having thicker skin," Leo admitted, leaning back, arms crossed, making his biceps flex. Vivian tried not to notice, but she couldn't deny Leo's sexiness. "But thanks for the heads up on how to manage the constructive criticism in the future."

"You and Burt just have different styles," Vivian remarked.

"Way different," Leo said, leaning toward her. "We don't see eye to eye on how to run this paper."

"Maybe not, but Burt wants you to succeed," Vivian said, distracted by the closeness of his body. She knew she should create some distance between them, but she leaned toward him instead as if pulled by some invisible magnet. "He knows that you're going to assert your beliefs and your views, and he's okay with that, because you have very deep convictions and you care. For you, the public has the right to know is not just some trite, journalistic cliché. You are fully committed to everything that you believe in, and that's something I've always loved about you."

"Is that so?" Leo said, grabbing her hand and gazing at her with those breathtaking blue eyes.

Disturbed by her slip, at how easily the words had tumbled from her mouth, Vivian cleared her throat. "What I meant was—"

A buzzy vibration against her hip interrupted her. "My cell. Just a sec," she told Leo as she slid off the desk and pulled the phone from the pocket of her Capri pants.

After entering her password, Vivian swiped her thumb across the screen a few times, accessing the text message she'd just received.

Vivian frowned as she read the message, confused and disturbed by the words.

"Viv?" Leo asked, concern in his voice. "You okay?"

"I don't know," Vivian said, disoriented. "It's just this text ..."

"What does it say?"

Shaking her head, Vivian said, "It's from—"

A sharp rap on the door made Vivian jump as the door opened.

"Sorry to interrupt, but there's a call for you, Vivian, on line five," Sophie Carter poked her head into the office. "Caller claims it's urgent and explosive. Says you will definitely want to talk to her."

"You can use my phone," Leo offered.

After thanking Sophie, Vivian pressed the number five and activated the speaker button so Leo could hear the call.

"This is Vivian Thomas," she said, distracted by the text she'd received and yet determined to maintain her professionalism. "How can I help you?"

"Actually, I'm going to help you, Ms. Thomas," said a throaty female voice, slightly smug. "I have a story that's going to sell a lot of newspapers for you."

"Well, selling newspapers is one of our primary goals," said Vivian, rolling her eyes as she caught Leo's skeptical gaze. "Whatcha got?"

"Not over the phone," said the smug woman. "In person only."

"I need to know a little bit more than you have a story that's going to sell a lot of papers," Vivian said, annoyed by the caller, a blatant attention seeker with nothing better to do. "I can't meet you in person unless I know it will be worth my while to do so."

There was a pause, and Vivian hoped the woman would hang up so she could get back to the text.

"It's about a scandal at St. Killian Bank," the woman said. "Clients are being screwed."

"You have proof of this?" Vivian asked, a bit more interested, noticing Leo scribbling something on a legal pad.

"That's why we have to meet," the woman said. "You need to see the evidence for yourself."

Glancing at Leo's note, Vivian saw it was a question he wanted her to ask. "How did you get this proof?"

"No more over the phone," the woman said. "You want this

story, and trust me, you do, then we need to meet in person. I'll tell you everything I know and give you all the evidence to prove I'm telling the truth."

Vivian glanced at Leo, and he nodded.

"Where do you want to meet?"

The woman dictated the details for the meeting, giving Vivian her address and phone number.

"I look forward to meeting you," said the woman.

"Wait a minute," Vivian rushed out. "What's your name?"

"Marlie," she said. "Marlie O'Neal."

"Well, that was intriguing," Leo said after Vivian ended the call. "What do you make of her story?"

"Not really sure," Vivian said. "But, if she works for the bank, maybe she's a whistleblower or a disgruntled employee who got fired for some reason."

"Or, maybe neither," suggested Leo. "Maybe she's a pissed-off customer who couldn't get a loan."

Vivian shrugged, once again distracted by the text, Marlie O'Neal fading into the background, becoming less important.

"You okay, Viv?" Leo asked.

"Thinking about the text I got," she admitted, though she knew it was risky to confide in Leo, to be lulled back into the comfortable friendship and familiarity they had once shared. "It was from a man named Jake Frankowski. Some private investigator Amal knew. His message said I need to talk to Amal. Do you know where she is?"

Chapter Twenty-Two

"I'd like to introduce myself," said a raspy but warm male voice with a slight twang. "I'm Jacob Frankowski, a good friend of Amal Shahin, and I'm calling because I'm trying to reach her. It's very important. I know you don't know me from Adam, Ms. Thomas, but Amal told me she was going to visit you, last time I talked to her, and I was able to track down your number."

"I see," Vivian said, taking a seat on one of the chaises on the terrace. "You're a private investigator, right? Amal's assistant told me about you. She said you were trying to reach Amal."

The dull ache in her neck still resisted her attempts to massage it away. Work had been tedious, made all the more tortuous because she'd spent the bulk of her time on the phone, chasing leads to nowhere, anxious and fidgety, thinking about the text from Jake Frankowski. She hadn't been able to concentrate and couldn't wait for the day to end so she could return Frankowski's call.

On the phone with him now, she remembered what had bothered her about his message. He didn't know Amal was dead. She was going to have to tell him, something she didn't want to do.

"It's important that I talk to her," he said, an anxious edge in his tone. "Is she there with you?"

Vivian opened her mouth, but she thought a sob might escape, instead of the words she didn't want to tell him.

"Hello?" Frankowski barked, a bit more panicked. "You still there?"

"Mr. Frankowski," said Vivian, taking a deep breath, trying not to break down.

"Jake, please," he said. "Mr. Frankowski is my father."

Vivian wanted to smile at his joke, a common quip men made to protest formalities, but knowing the horrible answer to his question about Amal, she could only brace herself for the inevitable. She dreaded talking about Amal being dead but resolved to be professional.

"Jake, um," Vivian started, and then cleared the hot mass from her throat. "Can you tell me why you needed to reach Amal."

"That's between me and Amal," he said. "Now, can you tell me if she's with you? Or, if not, can you get a message to her for me, please? Tell her to call me."

"I'm afraid I can't do that," Vivian said, glancing toward the Caribbean Sea. The sun had set moments ago, leaving behind dazzling streaks of orange and pink across the sky.

"What do you mean?" Frankowski asked.

Hesitantly, and haltingly, her heart thundering, Vivian said, "Amal is dead."

Silence ensued, a long protracted absence of sound, and Vivian feared the connection had been lost.

"Jake ...?" Vivian ventured, worried. "Mr. Frankowski?"

"Um, yeah ..." His voice was thin and high, and seconds later, he cleared his throat. "Yeah, I'm still here."

Vivian heard a hint of something in his gruff tone and recognized it as melancholy, a resigned remorse. Focusing on a palm tree, the breeze whispering between the fronds, she felt a poignant sadness in her chest. Jake Frankowski was very broken up about

Amal's death. Vivian guessed their relationship was more personal than professional. At once, she remembered Amal saying she might fall in love—with the right guy.

Had Amal been referring to Jake? Was he the right guy she could have fallen in love with?

"How did she die?" Frankowski asked.

"It was a hit-and-run accident, and the driver fled," Vivian said. "There was a witness, but he didn't provide very much information."

"Are the cops sure Amal's death was an accident?"

"Why would you ask that?" Vivian asked, her thoughts swirling, heading toward old speculations. She'd been forced to abandon her suspicions, but somehow, Vivian knew she'd never actually given up her belief that Amal's death had been intentional.

The conclusions of Baxter François had always given her reason to doubt. The detective had been convinced Amal was a hit-and-run victim. A tragic death, but nothing suspicious. Vivian supposed she'd never been persuaded by Detective François' opinions; she'd just accepted them because she'd been unable to dispute them.

"Ms. Thomas, I know Amal probably told you she was paying you a visit to catch up on old times, and that was somewhat true," Frankowski said, "but there was another reason why she went to St. Killian."

"What do you mean?"

"Amal went to that island to settle a score," Frankowski said. "And I think it got her killed."

Chapter Twenty-Three

"To settle a score?" Vivian jumped up from the chaise. "What does that mean?"

"Revenge," said Frankowski.

"Revenge?" Vivian echoed, confused, her heart pounding. "I don't understand."

"A few months before Amal went to St. Killian, she called me for a favor," he said. "She'd been receiving strange calls from some woman she didn't know."

"Who was the woman?"

"Can't remember her name," he said. "But, Amal was suspicious and asked me to check out the woman, find out what she wanted. Come to find out, the woman claimed that someone had stolen a significant amount of money from Amal. I checked out the woman's story. It was legit, so I told Amal."

"Oh my God," Vivian whispered, returning to the chaise. "Who stole Amal's money?"

"I wasn't able to find out," Jake said. "The snitch who was calling Amal wouldn't tell me, but she did say that the thief was in St. Killian."

"You think the person stole money from Amal and then fled to St. Killian?" Vivian asked, curiosity beginning to supplant her grief.

"Maybe. Not sure," the private detective mumbled, clearly distracted. "I think so."

"Tell me this," Vivian began, though she doubted she would get any clear, concise answers from the man. He was probably still reeling after finding out about Amal's death, desperately trying to process his grief and disbelief. "When you told Amal that someone had stolen money from her, what did she say?"

"She told me she was going to St. Killian to get her money back," Frankowski said. "I told her that direct confrontation might not be the best way to handle things, but you know Amal. She was not one to ever back down from a fight, and when she made up her mind to do something, she was going to do it, come hell or high water. She was going to get her money back from the person who stole it, by any means necessary, she said."

Disturbed, Vivian felt a chill go through her, despite the balmy breeze wafting across the terrace.

"When I found out about the money, I should have investigated it more myself," he said. "But, I had a lot going on. More clients than usual. Still, when Amal told me she was going to St. Killian, I was afraid of what she might do. I asked her to wait until things slowed down for me, and then I would go to the island with her. We could get to the bottom of things together. She didn't want to do that."

Vivian wasn't surprised. Amal was fiercely independent. Never relying or depending on anyone, she'd always preferred to handle her problems herself.

"It's my fault she's dead."

"What? No, Jake, don't say that," Vivian said. "It's not your fault."

Again, there was silence, and then Frankowski said, "Listen, the woman who was calling Amal lived in St. Killian, too. You need to tell the cops about her. They need to talk to her. I wish I could remember her name right now, but I'm a little ..."

"I understand," Vivian said, sympathetic toward his pain.

"The favor for Amal wasn't an official investigation, so it's not in my office database," he said. "All the notes are on my personal computer at home. I'm going to find the notes tonight, and I'll get back with you with the name of that woman."

After the call was over, Vivian leaned back on the chaise. Closing her eyes, she tried to gather her thoughts, to come to some conclusions about what the private investigator had told her.

It was a lot to understand, to process, to make sense of, and yet Vivian refused to allow confusion to deter her. Frankowski's revelations about Amal and her real reasons for coming to St. Killian had revitalized and re-energized her desire to determine the truth.

Galvanized, Vivian sat up and swung her legs off the chaise, placing her feet on the ground. She had to find out if Amal's death had been an accident, or if her best friend had been murdered.

She needed to find out more about the woman who'd called Amal. Who was she? How had she known Amal's money had been stolen? Did the woman live in St. Killian, as Jake Frankowski suspected? If so, Vivian would have to find the woman. She would have to convince the woman to give her the same information she'd given Amal—the name of the person Amal had come to St. Killian to confront.

The next step would be finding the thief, Vivian determined. If Amal had been murdered, then the killer might be the person who'd stolen Amal's money.

Chapter Twenty-Four

As soon as she walked into the *Palmchat Gazette* the next morning, Vivian sailed through the newsroom, rushed into the editor-in-chief's office, and closed the door behind her.

Leo had been on the phone, but her expression must have telegraphed her manic anxiousness, and he quickly wrapped up the conversation.

"What's the matter?" Leo asked, some of her anxiousness transferring to him.

"Amal was murdered," Vivian blurted out, voicing the conclusions she'd come to last night as she tossed and turned in bed, deducing and cycling through various theories based on everything Jake Frankowski had told her. "Her death was not an accident."

"What are you talking about?" Leo asked. "Why would you think that? The police—"

"The police were wrong," Vivian said, pacing back and forth in front of the large, file-strewn desk. "The police didn't have all the information. The police didn't know that Amal didn't come to St. Killian to visit me."

"She didn't?"

"Well, she did," Vivian said and then stopped pacing to take a breath. Staring at Leo, she said, "But, seeing me was just an afterthought. The real reason she came to the island was for revenge."

"Revenge?"

After another deep breath, Vivian grabbed Leo, pulled him over to the couch, and forced him to sit with her. Angling toward him, she divulged everything about the mysterious woman who'd called Amal, Amal's missing money, and Amal's plan to settle the score with the thief who'd stolen from her.

"What Frankowski told you is shocking," Leo said. "But, it doesn't prove Amal was murdered."

Vivian gaped at him. "Were you listening to me? How can you not come to the conclusion that Amal was deliberately killed."

"Viv, just think about something," Leo said.

"I don't want to think about anything except finding Amal's killer." Vivian jumped up and walked toward the desk. Facing him, she said, "Amal was murdered. She was not accidentally hit by some drunk who fled the scene. She was deliberately killed by the person who stole from her."

"Vivian, listen," said Leo, giving her a tone she recognized, a tone which irritated her, the placating voice of reason. Calling her Vivian instead of Viv was his coded warning, his way of saying don't go off half-cocked with half the information.

"I don't want to argue with you," Vivian said. "I just came to tell you that I need to take the day off, maybe a few days."

Suspicion in his gaze, Leo asked, "What are you going to do?"

"I'm going to do what I do best," Vivian said. "I'm going to get the truth about Amal's murder."

Chapter Twenty-Five

"Explain to me why we're here, again?" Leo asked, guiding Vivian's Range Rover into the gravel-and-weed parking lot of the Purple Gecko, the bar in Handweg Gardens where Amal's rental car had been abandoned a month ago, the night she was murdered.

Exhaling her annoyance, Vivian shook her head. "You're here because you insisted on driving me."

"Because I didn't want you to run off the road. You were so damn wired," he said.

"And for some reason, you didn't want me investigating by myself, even though I've done so plenty of times without you and with great success."

Secretly, Vivian's heart had fluttered when Leo told her he would be accompanying her to the Purple Gecko. The idea of Leo helping her investigate was tempting, ushering in memories of happy moments, idyllic times, she'd thought would last forever.

Forever hadn't been in their future, but she'd decided she didn't want forever with Leo anymore anyway.

Nodding, Leo said, "Yeah, that's right."

"I'm here to start my investigation of Amal's murder, to get information that will, hopefully, lead me to Amal's killer."

"And you believe her killer is the person who stole her money?" Leo asked.

"Based on what Jake Frankowski told me about Amal coming to the island to get revenge, yes, I do," Vivian said. "The mystery woman must have told Amal who'd stolen from her. Amal confronted that person, and then that person killed her."

"Why don't you just wait for Frankowski to give you the name of the mystery woman who was calling Amal," Leo suggested. "If she lives on the island, you can look her up and go talk to her."

"I plan to do that," Vivian snapped. "But, while I'm waiting to hear from Jake, I want to find out if any of the employees at the Purple Gecko know anything about the hit and run. One of them may have seen something they didn't tell the cops. Witnesses don't always want to get involved."

"If one of the employees saw something and they didn't tell the cops," Leo said, "what makes you think they would tell you?"

Affronted, Vivian glared at him. "Excuse me, but are you suffering from selective amnesia? Who got the interview with Charles Taylor? Who got the interview with Robert Mugabe? And who was able to get that former Boko Haram member to talk about—"

"Okay, all right," Leo said, laughing, looking impressed. "I forgot for a moment that I was sitting next to Vivian Thomas, the African warlord whisperer."

Stifling a chuckle, she punched his hard biceps. "Be serious."

"I am serious," Leo said. "Mugabe certainly didn't want to talk to me. So, come on. Let's go see what these Purple Gecko folks have to say."

"Wait." Vivian stopped Leo as he was opening the driver's door.

He glanced at her, brows lifted.

"What if one of the employees knows something, but I'm not able to get them to tell me? And what if that something they know is the key to solving Amal's murder? If I can't get the information, then whoever killed Amal might get away with murder, and it would be my fault because I wasn't able to—"

"Viv, stop it." Leo grabbed her hand and gave it a reassuring squeeze. "Don't sell yourself short, okay? Trust your skills and your instincts. You still got 'em. If one of the employees knows something, you'll be able to get the information out of them."

"I hope so," Vivian said, grateful for his comfort and support.

"I know so," Leo said, his hand moving toward her face, fingers landing lightly on her cheek, caressing.

Mesmerized by his smoldering gaze and the feel of his hands on her skin, Vivian fought the urge to lean forward until her mouth touched his. Instead, she pulled away and said, "Let's go."

Inside the seedy dive, Vivian paused as she took in the surroundings. A jukebox in the corner played Bob Marley's "Redemption Song." Booths lined the walls, and two men sat in a corner, engaged in an intense conversation. Glancing to the right, she saw a couple swaying slowly to the music, grinding their bodies against one another in an erotic display of passion.

A bartender leaned against the back of the bar, staring intently at a cricket game on the small black-and-white television mounted on the wall and didn't even notice them entering. Reaching the bar, she and Leo took a seat on the worn wooden bar stools.

Leo knocked lightly on the bar, and the bartender turned.

"Hey there. What can I get for you two beautiful people?" the bartender asked.

"You got Felipe beer?" Leo asked, casually.

"Of course! Good choice. One or two?" the bartender asked, raising an eyebrow toward Vivian. She nodded, and he turned to grab two beers and two glasses and placed them on the bar in front of them before turning his attention back to the television.

"How long has the game been going?" Leo asked.

"It's in the twentieth hour. You understand cricket?" the bartender asked.

"Yeah, I lived in Mumbai for almost a year. Fell in love with the sport then." Leo flashed a smile, and the bartender returned it.

"Most Americans don't have the patience for it," the bartender said, impressed. "You are the one exception."

Vivian poured her beer into the glass as she listened to Leo engage the bartender in idle conversation about the game and some of the professional stars of cricket. She wasn't remotely interested in a game she'd never understood, but she was grateful for meaningless small talk, which had a point—the banter gave Vivian a moment to get her thoughts together and determine which interviewing technique she would employ to get the answers she needed.

She couldn't blow it with the bartender. She'd almost messed up with Landon, and if not for Leo's wise advice, she might not have found out about the gun Amal had bought, a clue which made so much more sense now, knowing that Amal had come to St. Killian for revenge.

It was possible the bartender might have information she could take to Baxter François, a lead which would force him to reopen the investigation into Amal's death.

She had to ask the right questions. The skills she relied on to uncover the truth when she worked on a story would be the same skills she would depend on to get justice for Amal. But, what if she couldn't get the bartender to talk?

Vivian let out a shaky exhale, trying to remember who she was —a smart, sly investigative journalist. She'd always been successful because she was adept at getting people to tell her what she wanted to know. People opened up to her, sharing their secrets, spilling their guts. The bartender would be no different.

After Leo had introduced them to the bartender, Vivian said, "We're following up on the story about the hit-and-run victim found in the parking lot a month ago."

"That was a crazy night. This is a bad neighborhood, and crazy stuff happens here at the bar, but we never had no dead body in the parking lot before. I've never seen so many cops and ambulances here in all my years working at this bar," the bartender said.

"Did the police question you?" Vivian asked.

"I'll tell you what I told the police," said the bartender. "Don't know nothing. Didn't see the car. Didn't see who got hit. Didn't see nothing. Would have said something if I did."

Nodding, Vivian said, "Do you happen to remember, Mister ... I'm sorry, what is your name?"

The bartender hesitated slightly and then said, "Ratcliff."

"Nice to meet you, Mr. Ratcliff," said Vivian, giving him what she hoped was her non-threatening, trustworthy smile as she removed her cell phone from her purse. "What I was about to say was, the police were able to identify the hit-and-run victim. It was a woman named Amal Shahin. I have a picture of her. May I show it to you? I'd like to know if you remember seeing her in the bar?"

Vivian entered her code, accessed her photo gallery and showed the bartender Amal's picture.

"This lady got killed?" Ratcliff stared at the picture for several moments before shaking his head. "Damn shame to run over a beautiful woman like that."

"You recognize her?" Leo asked.

"No, I don't remember seeing her in the bar," the bartender said.

"Are you sure?" Vivian demanded, trying to temper her disappointment as she returned her phone to her purse.

"I wouldn't forget a woman like that," Ratcliff said. "At least, I don't think I would. But, so many people come here."

"It probably wasn't too busy on a Monday night, right? That's when the hit and run happened," Leo prodded.

"Monday would have been slow, but if there was a match on that night, I probably wouldn't have been paying much attention." The bartender shrugged, giving them a sheepish smile. "Even a beautiful lady might not have caught my eye, but Jameson would have noticed her."

"Jameson?" Vivian asked.

"Guy sitting over there." Ratcliff inclined his head toward the jukebox. "One of my regulars."

Vivian glanced right and saw the guy Ratcliff had indicated—a middle-aged man with silver-streaked dark hair.

"You think that guy Jameson was in the bar the night of the hit and run?" Leo asked.

"Probably was," Ratcliff said. "He comes in most nights during the week."

"You think he'll talk to us?" Leo asked.

Ratcliff shrugged, and then called out, "Mr. Jameson? Got a minute? These two beautiful people would like a word with you."

Sliding off the barstool, not bothering to wait for Leo, Vivian walked to Mr. Jameson's table.

"Excuse me, Mr. Jameson?" Vivian asked, pulling out the chair across from the man. "Do you mind?"

"Not at all." Mr. Jameson shook his head and smiled, a broad grin. He was a nice-looking man with a chiseled jaw and chin, sort of a silver fox. He was more polished and plastic than charming, though Vivian figured he did pretty well with the ladies.

"I'm Vivian Thomas from the *Palmchat Gazette*," she said, taking a seat. "I was wondering, did you hear about the hit-and-run accident that happened near the bar? About a month ago? The body was found in the parking lot of the Purple Gecko."

Slowly, Jameson nodded and leaned forward, resting his elbows on the scarred table. "I did hear something about that, yes."

"Well, I'm following up on that story and was hoping you would answer a few questions," Vivian said. "I won't take up too much of your time. "

"Take as much time as you need," said Jameson, his gaze flirty, dark eyes dancing with interest. Vivian could tell he found her attractive. In the past, she hadn't been above using her beauty to get an exclusive, but she wasn't in the mood to be coquettish.

"Does this woman look familiar to you?" Vivian held her phone so Jameson could see the photo of Amal, gorgeous in her sexy red dress. Purposely, she'd decided not to mention anything about Amal being the hit-and-run victim. Vivian didn't want to influence his memories. She didn't want him to think he should remember Amal just because he was a regular customer. She was only interested in what Jameson actually recalled, without any prompting from her.

"Should she?" Jameson asked, staring at Amal's photo, a mix of curiosity and salacious appreciation in his gaze.

"Does she?" Vivian pressed, wondering if she might have to change her interviewing tactics.

"May I ask what that woman has to do with the hit-and-run story?" Jameson asked and then swallowed the last of his drink.

"She was the woman who died," Vivian said, glancing at the photo of Amal and then back at Jameson.

"That's terrible," said Jameson, gaze concerned. "But I'm not surprised somebody ran her over."

Chapter Twenty-Six

Vivian glared at Jameson, her heart punching. "What do you mean, you're not surprised? Did you see the victim at this bar the night she was killed? Did you see her with someone? Did you see someone threatening her?"

"No, no," Jameson said, holding up his hands, shaking his head. "I don't recognize the woman. If she came into the bar the night she was killed, then it might have been before I got here or after I left, because I didn't see her. When I said I wasn't surprised, I meant because the parking lot is pitch-black once the sun goes down."

Her heartbeat returning to normal, Vivian sighed. "Oh."

"Don't know if you noticed it," Jameson went on, "but there are no street lights around this area. At night, there's a neon sign advertising the place, but half the time, it's flickering on and off. And the neon is purple, not the brightest color to begin with, you know."

Hands trembling from the sudden surge of adrenaline caused by Jameson's bombshell—which hadn't detonated, actually—

Vivian returned her phone to her purse, fighting frustration and disappointment.

"It's a shame she got hit," said Jameson. "But, it's damn near impossible to see when it's dark. I've been telling Ratcliff to get the owner to at least string a set of Christmas lights around the building, but—"

"Thank you for your time, Mr. Jameson," Vivian said and stood. Not bothering to say goodbye, she beckoned for Leo, still hanging back at the bar, letting her handle things, and then headed for the door.

"Jameson give you a lead?" Leo asked as they walked back to the Range Rover. Shielding her eyes from the scorching, late afternoon sun, Vivian shook her head.

Back in the SUV, Vivian slammed the passenger door closed and said, "That was a damn waste of time. The bartender didn't remember Amal, and neither did Jameson. Although, he told me something interesting. The Purple Gecko doesn't have any lights. It's pitch-black after dark."

"So you think maybe Amal was accidentally hit?" Leo asked, starting the Range Rover's ignition.

"It's wasn't an accident." She glared at him as she yanked the seatbelt and fastened it in place. "It was murder. Whoever ran her down like a dog took advantage of the fact that the parking lot was dark. I just wanted somebody to have seen Amal that night, but what would that have proved? What I need is for someone in that bar to have seen the car that hit her. I need the license plate number of the car that hit her, but how could anybody have seen anything with no street lights around?"

"And from what my sources at the police department told me, no surveillance cameras either," Leo said, making a wide circle around the gravel lot, steering back onto Sandy Coral Road, heading toward the main thoroughfare.

"All I know is that I can't waste any more time chasing false leads," Vivian said, pressing her head into the headrest. "I've already spent too long. A month has passed. I should have been trying to find Amal's killer. I shouldn't have let Baxter François convince me that Amal's death was an accident. He thinks that because it's easier for him. He doesn't have to investigate her death as an intentional homicide, which is what it was."

"Viv, don't beat yourself up," Leo told her, removing a hand from the wheel to grab her hand. "You didn't have all the information a month ago."

"But, somehow, I knew in my gut that Amal had been murdered," Vivian said. "I knew her death wasn't an accident, but I tricked myself into believing it was."

"You were grieving," Leo said. "You were trying to process the death of your best friend, trying to cope with losing her so suddenly and tragically. You can't fault yourself for—"

"It will be my fault if I'm too late," Vivian said, pulling her hand from his comforting grasp. "Amal's killer might have left the island by now. And if that's true, I don't know how I'm going to live with myself. How can I forgive myself if Amal's killer gets away?"

Chapter Twenty-Seven

Leo steered the Range Rover onto the outer coastal highway, a long rambling four-lane road that traversed the circumference of the island. Gentle slopes leading down to pristine beaches sped past in a blur. Trying to temper her frustration, Vivian listened to the calypso music playing softly from the radio as Leo drove along. The jungle passed before her eyes, entangled shades of greens and browns. She recognized this part of the island and knew they weren't headed in the direction of town or back toward the *Palm-chat Gazette.*

"Where are we going?" Vivian asked, looking over at Leo for the first time since they'd left the bar in Handweg Gardens.

"Not back to work," Leo said, stealing a quick glance in her direction. "You're too upset to get anything done. I need to get you calmed down before you go off and do something crazy."

Vivian stifled a smile at the familiar statement. How many times had Leo said similar words to her as she tracked down African warlords for her next story? She'd done so many things that were crazy in her pursuit of journalistic excellence. It was second nature to her to plunge into danger and worry about the consequences later. Luckily, she'd had Leo to stop her from going too far.

After fifteen minutes, Leo turned the SUV off the highway onto a narrow sand-covered road and drove for about a mile before one of the most beautiful beach bungalows Vivian had ever seen came into view. Pulling the Range Rover toward the side of the house, Leo parked the car and jumped out, heading to her side to open the door.

Vivian paused for a moment, taking in the tropical, yet modern, thatched roof and teakwood structure. The front door was made entirely of glass and offered an unobstructed view through the house to the glass patio door leading to the backyard lanai, which overlooked the aqua blue waters of the Caribbean Sea.

"Welcome to my little slice of paradise." Leo grabbed Vivian's hand to help her out of the SUV and then closed the door behind her.

Walking slowly behind him, Vivian noticed Leo's private beach peeking through the leaves of the grape trees surrounding his bungalow. Paradise indeed.

"You're renting this place?"

"I got a good deal and decided to buy it. Came with about four acres of land, plenty of space to expand and build in the future." Leo said, holding the front door open for her.

Vivian walked inside the one-room structure; every aspect seemed to blend naturally with the outside environment, while at the same time providing luxurious appointments inside to make secluded living desirable. The modern, casual furniture matched Leo's personality perfectly.

"Have a seat," Leo suggested as he walked into the small kitchen nook to the left of the front door.

"I can't sit right now." Anxiety and worry gripped her, as she paced across the room. Vivian wasn't sure if her agitated state was because of her stalled investigation of Amal's murder or from being close to Leo in his home. "I don't know what to do next. I have no leads and nothing else to follow up on to try to identify who murdered Amal."

"This is just a small setback, Viv."

"A small setback?" Vivian screeched. "You know it's more than that. What else do I have to go on? I thought I'd get some pivotal evidence from the bartender, something I could take to Baxter François to get him to focus on Amal's case again. But I failed."

"No, you didn't." Leo's voice wafted from the kitchen, his figure out of her view. "Don't forget the private investigator is going to call you with the name of the woman who lured Amal to this island in the first place. As soon as we get that name, I promise you, we'll find her and figure out who was stealing from Amal."

"I forgot about that." Relief washed over Vivian, and she felt dizzy from the pacing. Looking around the room, she saw Leo's king-sized bed, decorated in classic ivory and tan, to her right and a small loveseat to her left, against a wall next to an expertly carved teakwood credenza. With one last glance toward the bed, Vivian veered toward the left and sat on the couch, tucking her legs beneath her, and closed her eyes. Leo had always known how to calm her in times like these, helping to focus her thoughts rationally on the facts when she was erratic, prone to jump to extreme conclusions.

"Remember how you used to make me strawberry shakes to calm me down when we were in Africa?" Vivian said, thinking back on the meticulous manner in which Leo would chop the strawberries into small bits before mixing it into ice cream with a small amount of milk.

"Like this?"

Vivian opened her eyes. Leo held out a tall clear glass filled with a strawberry shake and a classic red-and-white-striped straw sticking out of the middle. Vivian shook her head and smiled. Not only had Leo remembered, but he'd also had provisions on hand right now when she needed it most.

"I can't believe you." Vivian reached for the shake, savoring the flavor as it slid across her tongue. The magic elixir was better than she remembered, and a wave of nostalgia washed over her, threatening to send her into an emotional tailspin.

Leo winked at her and walked back into the kitchen.

"You hungry?" he asked. "I can fix you a sandwich."

"That would be great."

Vivian glanced around the room. Besides the stylistic flair of the casual furniture, there weren't many personal items in Leo's home. She spotted the picture of Leo and his mother at his graduation from UCLA on the bed table next to an elegant ivory and crystal lamp. Looking over to the credenza, Vivian saw a laptop neatly placed in the center with his beat-up LA Lakers mouse pad, right next to his grandfather's sterling silver pocket watch. Each piece was extremely important to Leo, and he never moved without them. But there was one item to the left of the laptop that caused Vivian's breath to catch in her throat.

She stood from the love seat and walked over to the small hexagonal box made of beige-colored soapstone, intricately hand painted with safari motifs along the bottom edges. Vivian recognized the box immediately. She'd bought it for Leo on their first trip to Kenya at a local market, a week after they'd decided to date exclusively. She'd haggled with the feisty Kenyan in the marketplace for twenty minutes, just for sport, to get the price down. Vivian was stunned Leo had kept the box all this time. Had it become that important to him to carry wherever he went, just like the photo and the pocket watch?

Vivian glided her fingers along the smooth surface. Her heart swelled with love for Leo as the memories of exploring Kenya with him flooded her mind. Vivian lifted the lid. The interior was empty except for one rectangular paper, folded in sixths. Reaching inside, she took the paper out and flipped it over in her hand, wondering what it could be. The edges were stained, and the paper was yellowed in places from wear over the years. Portions were crumpled and then smoothed out again, abused from being opened and refolded many times over.

Opening the folds of the paper, Vivian's hands began to tremble as she realized exactly what it was.

Chapter Twenty-Eight

Leo reached from behind her, and Vivian jumped slightly from his touch.

Easing the pages from her hand, he gave her a plate of potato chips with a roast beef sandwich and then slowly folded the pages back to their original state. Turning the rectangular paper once in his hand, he placed it neatly back in the soapstone box and closed the lid.

"I don't know why I still keep this. It's not like I haven't memorized every line of this letter," Leo muttered.

The faded ink of words she wrote to Leo a year and a half ago when she walked out on him were permanently etched on those worn pages. Tears began to pool in Vivian's eyes, and she blinked to stop them from falling. Why did Leo still have the letter? What could he gain from keeping it with him all this time?

Vivian studied Leo's face, drained of color, as he stared painfully toward the small soapstone box. She was instantly aware of the toll he must have gone through when he returned from work to find she'd left him.

Vivian had fled to salvage her self-respect, her dignity, and her sanity. She couldn't allow herself to continue in a relationship where there were opposing views of what the future should be. She'd been self-absorbed, thinking only of her pain and bewilderment realizing that Leo would never marry her.

She hadn't allowed herself to think about what her departure would do to Leo. In her haste to leave, she realized now that Leo had been robbed of closure. He hadn't had the chance to respond to the criticism levied against him in the letter, to have his point of view heard. Saddened by how that must have made Leo feel, Vivian regretted walking out on Leo for the first time. She could have handled the collapse of their relationship better, more respectfully.

"Let's go outside on the veranda." Leo grabbed her hand, linking his arm with hers, and guided her out of the room onto the wooden deck. His demeanor was casual and relaxed again, the prior moment a fleeting memory tucked away in both their hearts.

Stepping out on the deck, Vivian paused to take in the view. An oversized round ottoman sat in the middle, surrounded by two chaise lounges, facing an endless view of the Caribbean Sea stretching toward the horizon.

Guided to the ottoman, Vivian sat down. Her mind reeled from Leo's keepsakes of their relationship, one representing the beginning and the other the end. Taking a bite of the sandwich, she chewed distractedly, her appetite vanishing as she struggled to understand why Leo had kept both items.

Leo was sitting on the opposite side of the ottoman, giving Vivian distance she wasn't sure she wanted right now. She wanted to ask him why he'd memorized the letter and kept it all this time inside the first gift she'd ever given him as his girlfriend. But would his answer change anything? Would it make the fact that he didn't believe in marriage any easier to understand? Not likely. Vivian already knew how his parent's disastrous divorce and Burt's ill-conceived advice had tainted Leo's views on the subject. What was the point of dredging up the history just to inflict old pain into this new situation?

Staring ahead at the water sloshing against the stairs leading down from the deck, Vivian was struck by the beauty of this location. "This is breathtaking," she said aloud, more to herself than to Leo.

"Yes, it is."

Turning toward Leo's voice, she realized he'd been staring at her this whole time. As Leo's eyes roamed over her face, she thought she would feel uncomfortable under his scrutiny. Instead, she felt at ease, a peace settling within her as they sat quietly with the sounds of the waves as their soundtrack.

"I tried to find you," Leo said, his voice hesitant, low and distant. His blue eyes vacant, Vivian imagined his mind had been transported back to the aftermath of his days without her.

"I went to D.C., but your boss at *The Washington Post* told me that you'd quit and didn't give an explanation. She had no idea where you'd gone."

Vivian looked away, sadness pooling within her chest.

"I called your mom. Her assistant made it clear that she would not be taking any of my calls." Leo shook his head and looked down at his hands. His voice had a slight tremor. "I felt lost. I needed to find you. To talk to you. So, I flew to Anchorage to see your dad."

"You went to see my dad?" Vivian was stunned. Her father had never told her about Leo's visit.

"You'd changed your cell phone number. I didn't know what to do. I just figured it was more likely that you'd be with him than your mom. I knew he wouldn't take my calls either, so I just showed up at his doorstep."

"What happened?"

"He told me that I'd screwed up and you no longer wanted me in your life. He warned me not to make trouble for you or hurt you ever again. He wanted me to leave you alone and go back to Africa." The hurt masking Leo's features was almost too much for

Vivian to bear. "He told me if he found out I was trying to reach out to you again, he'd make me regret it."

"Leo—"

"Viv, I never meant to hurt you. I thought I was—"

"Let's not do this. Not right now."

Vivian hung her head low, not willing to allow Leo's words to penetrate her defenses. It didn't matter what Leo's intentions were, his misguided views had destroyed their future, and she wasn't sure she'd forgiven him for that. She didn't want to hear him apologize. Not now. Not when the words didn't matter anymore.

Chapter Twenty-Nine

As the sun turned a hazy orange, Vivian and Leo sat in silence, listening to the waves, each absorbed in their own thoughts. She tried to think of nothing, but her mind was assaulted with memories of her relationship with Leo and how much she still missed what they had. Vivian rubbed her hand along her neck, trying to relieve the tension from Leo's revelations. She missed being with him, loving him, and being loved by him. The void his absence had created still hadn't been filled, and Vivian wondered again how long would it take for her to stop loving him?

A palpable change in the atmosphere prickled against her skin as she felt Leo's presence. The distance between them disappeared faster than she was ready for, and in an instant, he had moved to sit behind her, his thighs resting on the outside of hers, brushing them slightly. Touching her lower back softly, Leo began to knead small circles along her spine, increasing the pressure to alleviate the knots in her muscles. Relaxing as his hands worked their way toward her upper back, Vivian could feel the tension escaping from her body with each stroke.

Leaning back slightly, Vivian felt Leo's breath on her neck for a moment before his lips gently brushed against the nape of her neck, kissing her softly. With each kiss, he trailed a path down the side of her neck and across her shoulders, his mouth becoming more passionate with each touch. His tongue swirled against her skin lazily, without clear purpose, yet determined, sending her body into a spasm of ecstasy.

Rubbing his hands along her sides, Leo encircled her with his strong biceps, stroking her stomach lightly with his fingers before exploring her breasts. Playing with the lace fabric of her bra, he managed to release her nipples from the thin fabric, squeezing them with his fingertips, as a moan escaped Vivian's lips. An out-of-body experience took over as Vivian turned toward Leo, taking his mouth with her own.

Gently pushing him down against the plush ottoman, she straddled him and continued her exploration of his lips, basking in the taste of him. Leo pulled her closer, and she didn't resist, longing for the feel of his body pressed next to hers. Resting against his taut, muscular frame, she could feel herself giving in even though she knew this was wrong.

Making love to Leo again would be pointless. Nothing had changed in his views or hers. Sex with Leo would be akin to friends with benefits. Her heart would never accept him as just a friend. She couldn't give herself to him sexually without falling off the cliff of love for him all over again. She knew the end result of loving Leo. She still dealt with it every day—heartbreak.

Vivian jerked back, raising her body from Leo's, and stood up. Panting softly, she twisted her braids in her hands, laying them in a column over her left shoulder as she stared at him. Leo was aroused and looked confused, taken aback by the abruptness of the departure of her body from his.

"What's wrong?" Leo raised slightly, concern in his eyes.

"We can't do this. No matter how much I want you," Vivian said and then paused. "God, Leo I want you so much. But I can't allow myself to get involved with you again. Not like this. I don't want to get entangled in something that would be nothing more than a friends with benefits situation."

"What?" Leo frowned, sitting up. He reached for Vivian, but she pulled back. "Is that what you think I want? Viv, you have to know how I feel—"

A piercing ring from Vivian's cell phone permeated the air, and Vivian let out a quick sigh, thankful for the interruption. "I need to get that. It could be Frankowski about the woman who reached out to Amal."

Crossing the threshold into the bungalow, Vivian walked over to the couch and grabbed her purse, taking the cell phone from the front pocket. Glancing at the screen, she saw it was a local number and not the area code for Dallas where Frankowski lived. Pressing the green phone button, Vivian answered.

"Ms. Thomas, this is Marlie O'Neal. I know we were supposed to meet on Friday, but there's been a change in plans. Can you meet me right now?"

There was an urgency in the woman's voice that Vivian didn't remember from before. Had something happened to trigger this sudden need to talk now? Vivian didn't waste time pondering it. She needed the distraction from Leo, and this was the best one available.

"Of course. I'll leave right now." Ending the call, Vivian turned to see Leo standing in the doorway.

"Don't go. We need to talk."

"I can't. That was Marlie O'Neal. She needs to meet with me now to give me the scoop on the scam going on at St. Killian bank. I have to go."

Chapter Thirty

Thank God for timely interruptions, thought Vivian, hands gripping the wheel of her Range Rover as she drove west, fading sunlight in her eyes, giving the interior of the SUV a coppery glow.

If she hadn't gotten the phone call from Marlie O'Neal, who knew what would have happened between her and Leo.

As she sped down the two-lane highway, Vivian realized she had a phone call to thank for keeping her out of Leo's bed. She wanted to believe willpower, tenacity, and self-respect would have prevented her from falling into his arms, but she wasn't convinced.

It was possible she might have given in to his kisses and caresses despite her resolve to move on with her life and forget about her hopes of being with Leo. He was still impossibly sexy, and she was still irrevocably tempted by the idea of making love with him again.

Still, as she had told him, no matter how much she wanted him, she wasn't willing to entangle herself in a friends with benefits situation.

Forcing the thoughts of Leo away, Vivian listened to the instructions of the GPS voice navigating her to the home address of Marlie O'Neal, the woman who claimed to have explosive information about a scandal at St. Killian bank. Vivian still wasn't sure if she believed the woman or not. Was she a whistleblower or just a disgruntled employee with an ax to grind? Vivian didn't want to get in the middle of a dispute between an ex-employee and her boss. Nevertheless, the woman's claims had to be checked out. If Marlie O'Neal was legit, then the *Palmchat Gazette* might have another award-winning story.

After a few twisting turns, Vivian steered the Range Rover into the neighborhood of Avalon Estates. Serene and quaint, she knew it to be a neighborhood of large pastel-colored homes, mostly owned by ex-pats and rental property owners. With its palm-lined streets and manicured yards, it was one of the prettier residential areas.

Driving slowly, Vivian approached Marlie O'Neal's house, one of the bigger houses in a cul-de-sac of impressive properties. Again, she wondered if O'Neal was an employee out for revenge. The house was expensive. Ms. O'Neal might be an out-of-work vice president who hadn't appreciated being fired and was seeking to embarrass the bank with a bogus accusation.

Turning into the circular driveway, Vivian noted there were no cars parked in front of the house, but there was a two-car detached garage. She parked in front of the front door, cut the engine, grabbed her purse, and got out. As she headed up the steps to the wraparound porch, the balmy breeze carried hints of rose, allspice, and sea spray, an inviting fragrance that made her think of—

Vivian stopped and stared at the front door.

Was it open? Vivian took a few more steps closer, more curious than apprehensive. There was a noticeable crack between the door and the frame. Why? Had Marlie O'Neal forgotten to close her door? Vivian remembered a few days ago when she'd returned home to find her door ajar, thanks to the absentminded impatience of her maid, Cozette. She sighed, wondering if she should go inside the house.

Certainly, a slightly opened door didn't bother her. In Africa, it had been an invitation to investigate, but still, she'd made sure to be careful. Of course, in Africa, Leo had always been with her, and together, they'd had each other's backs, kept each other safe. Well, Leo wasn't here right now. And besides, she wasn't in the Sudan. She was in Avalon Estates, a lovely, quiet neighborhood, and sure, anything could happen here, but nothing probably would.

Undeterred, Vivian pushed the door back and stepped into a wide foyer, paved with travertine tile.

"Hello? Ms. O'Neal? Marlie?" Vivian called out, hoping she wouldn't startle the woman. "Are you here? It's Vivian Thomas from the *Palmchat Gazette*."

Vivian ventured from the foyer and into an open concept area where the living room, dining room, and kitchen shared the same large space. Furnished in muted earth tones, it seemed like a model home, tastefully and professionally staged to entice potential buyers.

"Ms. O'Neal, are you home?" Vivian angled through the couch and matching love seat, heading toward a vast, vaulted entryway, beyond which she saw a hall. "We were supposed to meet? The door was open, and—"

Glass shattered.

Vivian jumped and then froze. What the hell was that? "Ms. O'Neal?" Vivian said, her heart starting to pound. "Are you okay?"

She listened for a moment and then took a step.

Another crash, something heavy slamming into something large, sent Vivian's heart into her throat. The cacophonous thuds reminded her of Cozette's house cleaning, and yet something told her the crashing sounds in Marlie O'Neal's house weren't accidental. Something told her she'd walked in on some crime taking place. A burglary? Was Marlie O'Neal's house being robbed?

Get out of here, Vivian.

Deciding to return to her SUV and call the police, Vivian turned and walked back to the foyer. A few feet from the door, she pulled her phone from her purse, and—

Pain exploded in the left side of her head. Crying out, shaken, lights popping behind her eyes, Vivian pitched forward and stumbled into the wall. Sinking to her knees on the travertine tile, she fought the urge to get sick and glanced toward the front door.

Someone rushed by her. Vivian saw a blur of jeans and a dark T-shirt disappearing out of the house, out of sight.

Confused, desperate to get her bearings, Vivian crawled to the opened front door. Reaching up, she grabbed the handle and used it to struggle to her feet. Wobbly, she leaned against the door jamb. Her heart pounded as she stared outside, eyes drifting from the porch to the circular driveway.

She saw nothing. Whoever had rushed past her was gone. Gingerly, Vivian touched the spot where she'd been hit and then winced. Glancing at her fingers, she was thankful there was no blood. Head throbbing, she made her way back into the living room and sank down on the love seat. Who the hell had hit her? And why? Who had run out of the door? Marlie O'Neal? No, that didn't make sense. Why would Marlie agree to meet her just so she could knock her over the head? Besides, Vivian had the distinct impression that the person who'd run out had been a man.

Standing, Vivian stilled herself until the dizziness and nausea passed. She needed to call the police. First, she wanted to make sure Marlie O'Neal was okay.

Venturing down the hallway, Vivian searched for the would-be whistleblower. Her investigative mind always demanded a thorough search of every nook and cranny, every crease and crevasse. But it was a job for the police. She needed to call them and let the cops handle it.

Standing in the doorway of a bedroom she'd wandered into, distracted by the pain in her head, Vivian noticed something on the floor, near the foot of the king-sized bed. Heading into the room, she saw broken glass on the hardwood floors and dresser drawers yanked out, clothes strewn across the floor. The room looked as though it had been tossed. Had someone been looking for something?

Blinking to focus her vision, Vivian stared at the object on the floor.

No, not an object. A woman. Sprawled on her back, arms and legs akimbo, eyes staring at the ceiling.

"Oh God ..." Vivian whispered, lurching to her knees next to the woman, pressing two fingers against the cool neck. Was this Marlie O'Neal? Vivian had no idea. But, if it was Marlie, then she was dead.

Chapter Thirty-One

The ringing was distant, muffled against the haze in her mind, growing louder as Vivian tried to force her eyes open from her deep slumber. Where was that noise coming from? As one eye opened slightly, she saw the time on the microwave in the kitchen. It read 1:23 p.m. She'd been asleep for over fifteen hours.

Vivian touched the left side of her skull gingerly, a dull pain radiated from the small lump on her head. The ringing continued, more insistent and Vivian realized it was her doorbell. Wiping her mouth, she sat up. Relieved that the dizziness and nausea were long gone, she pressed her way up from the couch and walked to the front door, opening it.

It was Leo.

For a moment, she felt dizzy, like she'd been hit in the head again from the sight of him. Leo oozed sex appeal, even as he stood before her in baggy jeans and muscles bulging through a retro Ghostbusters white graphic T-shirt.

Her body was instantly alert, and she took a deep breath, hoping the frenetic electricity coursing through her veins would subside.

Leo stared at her, assessing without words, before he pulled her into his arms, burying his head in her neck. The embrace shocked her as she could feel relief pouring from his body.

"Are you okay? Did you go to the hospital and get checked out?" Leo's words were muffled and warm against her skin as he tightened his embrace.

"Yes, I did," Vivian said, breathless.

Releasing her, Leo crossed the threshold and closed the door, then grabbed her hands, leading her to the couch. As they sat down, he wrapped his arms around her again and kissed her temple tenderly.

"What did the doctor say?" Leo's expression was concerned. Vivian guessed he still needed reassurance that the tragic circumstances of last night hadn't left a toll on her.

"Small contusion from the blow, but no concussion. I was safe to go home and resume normal activities," Vivian said as she tucked her feet into the cushions of the couch and burrowed her head against Leo's chest. She had resisted every urge to call him last night. She was no stranger to dangerous ordeals. Through them all, Leo had been a constant presence. Dealing with Marlie's death alone had been harder than she thought, a reminder of Amal's death a month ago. It felt natural and right for him to be here with her right now, comforting her.

"Tell me what happened last night. When I saw the morning edition, I couldn't believe Beanie had published that crap article. Then he told me why he'd taken a vague slant on the whole incident. You were the acquaintance that found Marlie's dead body."

"I asked Beanie not to mention that I was there." Vivian thought back on her 9-1-1 call after she'd found a body, lying still on the floor. Her head had been foggy, and she felt disoriented as she'd searched through the woman's belongings before stumbling upon the access badge, still clipped to the waistband of Marlie's pencil skirt. Staring at the photograph of the smiling brunette with freckles, her eyes had drifted to the words "St.

Killian Bank" above the photo and "Marlie O'Neal" etched below.

"I'm glad," Leo said. "Beanie told me you called him right after reporting the murder to the police. By the time he arrived, the cops were already on the scene."

"The police took my statement and gave a quote to Beanie for his story before Beanie drove me to the hospital."

Leo rubbed Vivian's arm lightly, absently kissing the top of her head, sending another jolt of electric energy through her body. "Did you even get a chance to talk to Marlie about the scandal at the bank?"

"No, she was already dead when I arrived. The door was slightly open, which I knew was strange. I went in any way."

"Viv—"

"I know I took an unnecessary risk. I just never thought I'd find a dead body in the house." Vivian recounted her journey through Marlie's home, the commotion coming from the bedroom before she decided to leave and call the police.

"Just when I was about to do the right thing, that's when I got hit on the head," Vivian continued.

"Did you see who hit you?"

"No. Everything happened in a blur, but I could tell it was a man. After I got my bearings, I went into the bedroom, and that's when I saw the place had been ransacked and Marlie's dead body was on the floor."

"Damn," Leo said frowning, his jaws clenching as he stared toward the window. "And how long did it take you to get to Marlie's house after she called?" Leo asked.

Vivian suspected he was trying to construct a timeline of events. Could Marlie have known that the killer was after her? Was that why she was insistent on meeting with Vivian last night?

"A little less than an hour," Vivian responded. "She could have been home when the guy broke in, or she could have walked in on him already tossing the place."

"Well, Beanie got an update from our source at the police station while I was driving over here. Apparently, Detective François thinks Marlie knew her killer."

"Really? Why?" Vivian was perplexed.

"There was no signs of forced entry. On top of that, Marlie had quite the collection of expensive jewelry with some pieces worth thousands of dollars."

"None of which was stolen by the perp," Vivian guessed.

"And they found her purse in the closet with seven hundred dollars inside and all her credit cards. None of these items were taken either."

"What are they thinking? Some domestic dispute?" Vivian asked.

"Exactly."

Vivian drummed her fingers against her thigh.

"What's your gut telling you?" Leo asked.

"I just can't shake the sense that the killer was looking for something in particular. He was tearing the place apart after he'd already killed Marlie," Vivian said. "Marlie claimed she had proof of the scandal at St. Killian Bank. Maybe the guy who broke into her place was looking for that proof?"

"You may be on to something," Leo said. "If the guy who broke into Marlie's house knew that she had some evidence against him, he might have killed her to keep her from giving it to you."

"Just wish I knew what the scandal at the bank was about or what type of proof she had."

"Maybe that's for the best that you don't know."

"Why do you say that?" Vivian asked, pulling back from Leo's chest to look into his crystal blue eyes. The intensity of his gaze arrested her, and it took every ounce of her resolve not to swoon.

"If I had known that Marlie's scandal would put your life in danger, I never would have forgiven myself for letting you go off to see her alone."

"I'm fine. Stop being melodramatic." Vivian slapped at Leo's chest, trying to lighten the mood.

"That guy killed Marlie, and he could've killed you," Leo said, the conviction in his voice startling her. "Do you know what that would have done to me? I don't want to exist in a world that you aren't living in."

"You didn't lose me. I'm still here." Vivian immediately regretted her choice of words as a sly smile began to spread across Leo's face.

Leaning in toward her, Vivian felt Leo's lips press against hers, gently parting her mouth to allow full access. Heat flushed Vivian's skin as she fell into the abyss of Leo's tender kisses. Pulling back after a series of deeper kisses, Vivian inhaled shakily.

"We've got to stop doing this."

"I don't just want to be friends with benefits with you, Viv. I want things to be like they were before."

"That's the problem. How we were before is not enough for me." Pushing away from Leo, Vivian stood to put some distance between them.

"You don't understand. We need to talk about us."

"There is no us. Not anymore. I understand exactly how and why we got to this point."

"Things are different now."

"No, they're not." Vivian's head began to throb as she felt tears floating to the surface of her eyes. "Can you just go? I can't deal with this right now."

Leo rose slowly, defeat in his strides as he walked toward the door. Stepping outside, he turned to look at her.

Vivian paused, her heart pounding afraid of what he was about to say.

"Viv."

"Yes, Leo."

"I love you."

Chapter Thirty-Two

Leaving the newsroom, Vivian crossed the small vestibule and exited through a set of walnut doors into the *Palmchat Gazette* lobby, a spacious area with lots of natural light and wicker furnishings. Vivian gave a quick wave to Millie, the efficient, industrious eighty-something receptionist, who, minutes ago, had buzzed to let her know she had a visitor waiting in the lobby—someone named Renee Greenwood.

Vivian headed to the sitting area, where a young woman perched on one of the couches, facing the pedestrian traffic outside the ceiling-to-floor windows.

Standing in front of the woman, Vivian took in the cherubic frame, strawberries-and-cream skin, and short platinum curls. Her white sundress barely contained her ample bosom and hardly covered her plump thighs.

She didn't recognize the woman and couldn't image why the zaftig Marilyn Monroe wanted to see her, but Vivian was glad for the chance to maybe, hopefully, have something to focus on besides Leo.

Or, more precisely, Leo's bombshell confession.

"I don't just want to be friends with benefits with you, Viv."

She should have stopped him right there. She'd known the conversation was heading into a dangerous territory, with no way to reverse course. She should have reminded herself of her resolve to move on with her life. Struggling to remember her three a.m. epiphany, she'd tried to brace herself against the onslaught of emotions from his presence.

She shouldn't have allowed him to comfort her, to kiss her, and hold her, but it had felt so right, so natural, being in his arms.

"I love you."

Vivian had been shocked by the words but not because Leo had spoken them. She knew how he felt about her, which was the same way she still felt about him. The love between them was still alive. Vivian had been surprised at how hopeful the sentiment had made her, even though she knew the hopes were unreliable. The hopes would end up dashed—again. She knew better than to wish and dream and long for those old fantasies and fairy tales she'd given up on, but she couldn't help herself.

"I want things to be like they were before ..."

Vivian wanted the same thing, but she hadn't been able to tell him that yesterday. Unprepared for his heartfelt admission, Vivian had faked a headache and exhaustion. Leo hadn't pressed her, but thankfully had gone along with her pretense and agreed to leave so she could rest.

Rest. What a joke. After Leo had left her condo, she'd cycled through so many emotions—joy, anger, grief, excitement, shock, suspicion—that it had taken two and a half glasses of wine to calm down.

After ruminating over the situation with Leo for the rest of the afternoon and into the night, she'd woken up this morning with Leo still haunting her thoughts.

"Renee Greenwood?" Vivian extended a hand. "I'm Vivian Thomas. How can I help you?"

"Oh, Ms. Thomas, hi," the woman said, standing, wobbly in her wedge heels. "Yes, I'm Renee Greenwood. It's good to meet you. I always read your articles. They're really good."

"Well, thank you," Vivian said. With an open palm, she invited the woman to sit again, as she sat on the opposite end of the wicker divan. "Now, why did you want to see me?"

"Yes, I um … have something for you," said Renee Greenwood. "A friend of mine wanted you to have it. She would have given it to you herself, but …"

Vivian noticed a resigned sadness in the woman's gaze which reminded her of the sadness she kept hidden away.

Her incurable affliction; it wouldn't kill her, but unless she resolved to soldier on, it might adversely affect her life. The sadness would remain because Amal was gone. Vivian was learning to manage it, to suppress it and stop it from paralyzing her, but there were still times when the sadness got the best of her, reminding her that life would never be the same. Amal's death had altered her existence.

"Do I know this friend of yours?" Vivian asked, allowing curiosity to suppress the melancholy threatening to overtake her.

"I think you knew her."

Knew her, Vivian noted, catching the past tense.

"You wrote a story about what happened to her."

Vivian frowned. "I did?"

"Well, maybe you didn't write it, but there was a story in the *Palmchat Gazette* about her," Renee Greenwood said. "Marlie O'Neal. She was killed by someone who broke into her home."

Vivian nodded, remembering Marlie O'Neal, lying on the bedroom floor, strangled to death. The killer had attacked Vivian before fleeing the house, a murderer she couldn't identify, someone who'd ransacked Marlie's bedroom, who'd been looking for something, possibly the evidence Marlie had planned to show her.

"…what really happened," Renee Greenwood was saying.

Focusing her attention on the pneumatic blonde, Vivian said, "I'm sorry?"

"Do you know what really happened to Marlie?" Renee asked. "The cops questioned me, her family, and other friends, but they didn't give a lot of details. Just said they were still gathering evidence, still investigating."

"Sometimes it takes a while for the police to figure out the truth," Vivian said. "They don't want to compromise the investigation by revealing crucial information before they've had a chance to look into it thoroughly."

"I've heard sometimes cops will tell reporters stuff off the record," Renee Greenwood went on. "Stuff they don't want in the papers. Did the cops ask you guys to keep some stuff off the record?"

"Stuff like what?"

"Like who was the acquaintance who found Marlie?" Renee asked. "Wasn't me. Wasn't any of Marlie's other friends."

Holding the woman's searching gaze, Vivian decided, for now anyway, not to reveal herself as the acquaintance mentioned in the article. Renee would have questions, and Vivian didn't have all the answers. She didn't want to disappoint the woman.

"Renee, I'm sorry for your loss," Vivian said and quickly directed the conversation back to its original purpose. "What did Marlie want you to give me?"

Renee Greenwood opened her purse. She delved a hand inside the large red leather pouch, pulled out a tiny purple flash drive and gave it to Vivian. "This is what she wanted you to have."

"A flash drive." Vivian inspected it. "Did she tell you what was on it?"

Shaking her head, Renee said, "She just wanted me to keep it for her. She told me she needed to give it to Vivian Thomas."

"When did Marlie give you the jump drive?"

Renee Greenwood looked at the ceiling. "I think it was maybe a week before Marlie was killed. Maybe, I'm not really sure. Four or five days, maybe?"

"The day she was killed, Marlie and I were supposed to meet," Vivian said, doubtful of Renee's claims, although not sure if she should be skeptical just yet. "If she wanted to give me the jump drive, then why did you have it?"

"Marlie could be really spastic and absentminded, not a good combination," Renee explained. "She said she might accidentally misplace the jump drive before she could deliver it to you, so she wanted me to keep it. She was supposed to get it back from me when she was ready to give it to you, but that didn't happen."

Vivian asked, "Did you ask her what was on the jump drive?"

Rolling her eyes, Renee said, "I didn't want to know. It's probably porn."

"Porn?" Vivian echoed, shocked and skeptical. Had Marlie wanted to expose a sex scandal at St. Killian Bank? Marlie said customers were being screwed. Vivian assumed she was using screwed as an idiomatic expression, meaning the customers were being cheated or defrauded, but maybe Marlie had been using the word screwed literally.

"I don't know for sure," Renee said, sheepish, as though embarrassed by what she'd said. "I just said that because this guy Marlie was hooking up with has been calling me, asking me if I know anything about some files that Marlie saved to a flash drive. I figure this douche is talking about the flash drive Marlie wanted you to have."

"Did you tell him you have the jump drive?"

"He keeps leaving messages and texts on my phone," Renee said, "but I haven't called him or texted him back. I don't plan to. He's a total skeeve. Like, he's married, right? But, has that stopped him from hooking up with all the admins in operations? I tried to tell Marlie not to trust that toad."

"Who are the admins in operations?"

"The administrative assistants in the operations department," Renee said. "That's where I work. Marlie worked there, too."

"And does the skeeve work there?" Vivian asked.

"Grant Stone is his name." Renee made a face of disgust. "He's one of the VPs at St. Killian Bank. Completely smarmy. I don't know what Marlie saw in him."

Vivian glanced down at the jump drive in her palm.

"I'll tell you everything I know and give you all the evidence to prove I'm telling the truth."

Could the jump drive be the proof Marlie had wanted to show her? Did the jump drive contain evidence related to the scandal Marlie had claimed was going on at St. Killian Bank?

"Another reason why I thought it was porn," said Renee, cutting into Vivian's thoughts, "is because it's password protected."

Vivian almost groaned. "Let me guess. You don't have the password."

"No, sorry," Renee said, apologetic. "Knowing Marlie, the password could be anything."

"That's okay," Vivian said, her irritation tempered when she remembered Stevie Bishop's cousin, rumored to have hacked into the private email of the governor of the Palmchat Islands. A simple flash drive would be no problem for him. "I think I know a way to get the information."

"I hope it's not porn," Renee said, her smile sheepish as she stood, signaling the end of their conversation. "And I hope it's not ..."

"What?" Vivian prodded, rising from the couch.

"I hope it's not something that she wasn't supposed to have," Renee said, shaking her head, flustered. "What I mean is, whatever is on that jump drive, I hope it didn't get her killed."

Chapter Thirty-Three

"Vivian, it's Jake Frankowski. Took some digging, but I found the name of the woman who'd reached out to Amal and set her off on a quest for revenge."

Sitting on a wooden bench in the middle of lush emerald grass and gardens filled with hibiscus, yellow bells, and jasmine, Vivian was startled by the call from Jake. She had left her condo early this morning for a ten-mile run ending at the one-hundred-year-old Fort Killian, an unfinished construction slated for the defense of the Palmchat Navy armory that was turned into a park thirty years ago.

The run was supposed to clear her mind from the onslaught of confusion created by Leo. She'd spent yesterday avoiding him at work, knowing that making it to the weekend would give her the separation she needed to figure out how she felt about his declaration of love.

Jake's call was a reminder she had more important things to deal with, like getting evidence to prove Amal's death was not an accident. Piecing together the fragments of who killed Amal was where her focus should be.

"Who is it?" Vivian asked, anxious to get another lead.

"Woman by the name of Marlie O'Neal," Jake answered. "First time she called Amal was ..."

As he continued to speak, his words were swallowed in the roaring of her mind as she struggled to make sense of it all. Staring toward one of the gray tarnished cannons sitting on a garrison in a corner of the pentagonally shaped fort, Vivian couldn't believe what she'd just heard.

"Wait ... did you just say Marlie?"

"Yes. M-A-R-L-I-E O'Neal was the woman who'd said someone had stolen a significant amount of Amal's money." Jake reiterated.

"I know her," Vivian said.

"You know Marlie O'Neal?" Jake demanded, his tone incredulous. "How?"

"A few days ago, she called the newspaper with a scoop on customers getting screwed at St. Killian Bank," Vivian said, hoping to calm his ire. "I was meeting up with her to get information for a story."

"Did she mention anything about Amal?"

Vivian said, "Marlie O'Neal was killed before I had the chance to talk to her."

"What the hell?"

"She was murdered in her home the same day she and I were supposed to meet," she said. "I was the one who found her body. She'd been strangled."

"Well, this ain't the movies. It takes several minutes to strangle someone to death by hand, and it's not worth an intruder's time to take that long if they believe they need to kill. Do the cops think she knew her attacker?"

"I think so," Vivian said. "The cops said there was no sign of forced entry."

"You think Marlie's death had something to do with the information she had about customers getting screwed at the bank?"

"Yeah, I do," Vivian admitted. "I'm finding it hard to believe all of this is a coincidence, especially since Marlie was trying to warn both me and Amal about a crime that involved people's money."

"Marlie tried to give the evidence to Amal," Jake said. "We don't know for sure if Amal got it or not, but Amal does come up dead. Marlie still has the evidence, so she decides to take what she knows to the newspaper."

"But Amal bought a gun. I think Amal did find out who had stolen from her and that's why she got the weapon. You know, to force that person to give her money back." Vivian added, an uneasiness settling within her core as the reasons for Marlie's and Amal's deaths coincided.

"Amal confronts the thief, and instead of giving her back the money, the bastard runs her over like a dog in the street."

Vivian bristled at Jake's crude reference to Amal's death. The wind picked up, blowing her braids into her face as she stared at the panoramic view of town from the top of the fort. She watched the private yachts maneuver into the harbor, waiting for her grief to subside.

"Now, knowing Amal, she probably made it her mission to let this guy know who her source was to prove she knew he was the thief," Jake continued.

"And Marlie O'Neal became his next target. Whatever she wanted to tell me was probably the same information she gave to Amal." Vivian constructed the pieces in her mind, convinced that Marlie's death was the bridge to finding Amal's killer.

The jump drive. Renee said Marlie wanted Vivian to have it.

What was on the jump drive? Could the contents of the device hold the truth about who killed both women? Stevie's cousin was hacking into the jump drive and hopefully would have the contents available for her soon. But something was still bothering her about both Amal's and Marlie's actions.

"Jake, what I don't understand is why they didn't go to the cops. Amal could have taken the evidence to the police and had the thief arrested instead of orchestrating her own vigilante justice that led to her death. Marlie, too. Why go to the newspaper instead of the police?" Vivian frowned.

"The cops are the last people Amal would have wanted to be involved in this matter ..."

"Why do you say that?" Vivian raised her voice, unsure of what Jake was dancing around. What had Amal been involved in? Why wouldn't she have sought help from law enforcement? Her best friend could still be alive now if she hadn't insisted on taking matters into her own hands.

"The truth is, there are parts of Amal's life that she kept hidden from all of her loved ones. Things y'all couldn't know. It was for your own protection."

"What the hell does that mean? She was my best friend! We had no secrets from each other." Vivian looked around the fort worried that someone had heard her yelling, but the area was empty except for a few pelicans walking through the sculpture garden.

"You sure about that?" Jake asked, doubt dripping from his words.

Vivian hesitated, not wanting to respond to his question. All of the things Amal had done in St. Killian were kept a secret from her. Vivian was struck again by how much she didn't know about one of her oldest and closest confidants.

"Tell me what Amal was up to," Vivian said softly, trying to prepare herself for the truth Jake was going to unleash.

"She was a drug dealer."

Chapter Thirty-Four

Vivian drove along the coastal highway, vision blurred from crying as the raspberry-pink beaches and aqua water whizzed by. She had been on the road for almost an hour, caught up in her thoughts and not paying attention to where she was going.

"No one is ever going to make a fool of me again."

Those words haunted Vivian, reminding her that she never really knew her best friend. Amal's raw, unbridled ambition had led her to a life of crime, driven by desperation to attain the money and prestige she coveted.

Vivian had stumbled through the stone-covered tunnels of Fort Killian in a daze, reeling from Jake's tale of Amal's secret life.

"I like to operate on both sides of the law. I don't personally commit any crimes, but everybody needs someone investigated from time to time. Who am I to judge what they choose to do for a living?" Jake had told her as he explained how he had met Amal. One of his clients had asked him to look into Amal's background before agreeing to bring her into the fold of the illegal prescription drug business.

As Jake had gathered intel on Amal, they'd developed a

mutual attraction. One that led to a continued relationship even after his job was done. Amal never asked him to get involved with her drug dealing, and he didn't judge her for her life choices.

Jake's recap of Amal's last year replayed in her head. About a year ago, he'd learned that Phoenix Medical Spa was deeply in the red after its first year in operation. Amal had been struggling to maintain a consistent clientele and establish a regular cash flow stream for her business. The medical spa market was saturated in Palm Beach, and she'd overestimated her abilities to make Phoenix stand out from the rest. Determined not to be a statistic of businesses that fail in the first year, Amal had tapped into an underground collective of shady pharmacists, doctors, and black market prescription drug dealers and convinced them to allow her into the group. Phoenix was the perfect legitimate front to supply the pampered Palm Beach elite with the recreational prescription medication they desired.

"Once she cleared my investigation, I reported back to the group, and Amal became the primary distributor of prescription opiates in her area. She had a reliable network providing regular inventory of Oxycontin, Vicodin, and codeine to her facility," Jake had explained.

The rumors of the extra services available from Phoenix Medical Spa quickly spread through the country clubs of the wealthy Palm Beach society. In less than three months, Amal had made a million dollars. She'd chartered a private plane to take herself and Jake to Cuba for a celebration. On the way back, they'd stopped off in the Cayman Islands, where Jake suspected she'd set up a series of offshore accounts to hide her illegal funds from the government and law enforcement.

"Amal gained power in the group, adding more distribution channels to get product for her spa and for the others. She had a knack for sniffing out shady and unethical doctors who'd help supply in small quantities for a kickback," Jake had explained.

Spreading out the inventory reduced the likelihood that Amal or her associates would be caught.

The millions kept rolling in over the months with no signs of stopping, Jake had told her. But Amal got nervous when the phone calls from Marlie started. She wasn't sure if the calls were legit or a cover for some police sting designed to bring down her whole operations.

"That's the only time she asked me to do a job for her," Jake had said. "Find out why the woman was contacting her. I just wish she'd waited for me to help her deal with the information she got. She might still be alive today."

Jake's voice had been full of regret and remorse, while Vivian had been seething. Amal would still be alive today if she hadn't felt the need to cut corners and turn to crime to pad her pocketbook. Every illegal move she'd made for the sake of saving her business had led to her death.

Vivian understood why Amal had to handle the stolen money alone. She couldn't go to the cops without revealing that another criminal had stolen her own ill-gotten gains. Confiding in Vivian wasn't an option for Amal either. She would never have agreed to help Amal if she'd known how Amal had amassed her wealth.

Vivian shook her head in disgust. The life her best friend led was more dangerous than she'd ever realized. As much as she'd wanted to dispute Jake's claims, she knew the man had no reason to lie. He had loved Amal in his own way; it was obvious from how he spoke of her. He gained nothing from slandering her. Vivian had to face the disappointing reality that her best friend was not the person she thought she was.

Pushing the Range Rover faster, Vivian wiped a tear from her cheek. Disillusioned, she knew the truth about Amal's life threatened to destroy the memories of the woman she'd loved like a sister. Vivian wasn't sure what to do anymore. Was it worth her time and effort to hunt down the murderer of her drug-dealing best friend?

Desolate from Amal's actions, Vivian wasn't able to reconcile the woman she thought she knew to this criminal mastermind and drug dealer to the pampered rich that Jake had described. Turning off the coastal highway onto the small sandy road, Vivian drove another mile before parking the SUV.

As she walked toward the house, the door opened, and Leo stepped out on the portico, worry in his eyes. Falling into his arms, Vivian wailed as the full weight of the truth threatened to crush her.

Chapter Thirty-Five

Sitting at her desk in the study on the second level, Vivian leaned forward in her leather chair. Anxious to listen to the message again, for the third time, she pushed the PLAY button on her answering machine.

"Ms. Thomas, it's, um, Renee Greenwood," she said, panic palpable in the rushed tone. "We spoke a few days ago when I gave you the flash drive that Marlie O'Neal wanted you to have. Well, I found out the flash drive contains sensitive, confidential information about the bank that Marlie illegally downloaded. It has info she wasn't supposed to have access to which means she stole it which means she committed a crime. That's why Grant Stone was looking for the file, so can you please return it to him? He says I can get into trouble for giving you stolen information, and he said your newspaper could get into trouble too if you don't return the flash drive. He's going to get the cops involved, so can you please return the flash drive? I don't want to lose my job."

The message ended, almost abruptly.

Renee Greenwood was scared. Grant Stone had put the fear

into her, but Vivian wanted to tell Renee there was no need to worry about losing her job or Stone's threats of calling the cops.

Grant Stone had lied to Renee.

Staring at the purple flash drive extending from the side of the computer, Vivian wasn't surprised the man wanted it, considering the information on the files. For the past two hours, Vivian had been studying the contents—thanks to Stevie's cousin—and had come to a disturbing conclusion.

The contents of the jump drive had been the motive for Marlie's murder.

Galvanized by her speculations, Vivian grabbed the phone to call Leo but then stopped herself, wary of allowing herself to rely on him—again.

Yesterday, following the call from Jake Frankowski, Vivian's mind had been in shambles. The shock of his unbelievable claims had been too difficult to process. His incredulous revelations about Amal had depressed and offended her.

Disheveled and distraught, Vivian had fled for dear life to the only person who could give her the solace she craved, the sanctuary she needed, the only person who could hold her and keep her together even as she was unraveling—Leo.

After a torrent of tears, and with Leo's gentle encouragement, Vivian repeated the private investigator's damning words, whispering the accusations against her best friend, the woman who was closer than a sister. Repeating Jake's confession, Vivian had experienced the shock all over again. Another emotion accompanied the disbelief—shame. Vivian had been embarrassed, realizing her best friend was someone she hadn't really known.

Vivian remembered falling asleep in Leo's arms, lulled into a fitful slumber by his soothing words. The next morning when she woke up, she found herself in his bed—alone. Staring into the living area, she saw Leo asleep on the couch. Though Vivian was tempted to make coffee and breakfast, waking him with the smell of bacon and eggs, she instead wrote a quick goodbye note and slipped away.

She'd been too mortified to face him.

Thinking of her breakdown now, Vivian cringed, remembering how she'd run to LEO. He'd broken her heart, but she'd clung to him as though he were a lifeline, desperate to be held together by the man who'd once torn her entire world apart.

Still, Vivian wasn't sure she regretted her actions. She couldn't deny needing Leo in what had seemed her darkest hour. Soliciting his reassurance might have derailed the progress she'd made in her quest to give up the fantasies of them being together. No matter what, the end of their relationship didn't mean they weren't still friends. There was no shame in relying on a friend.

Vivian exhaled and dialed Leo's number. As the ringing blared in her ear, a fissure of worry sliced through her. Consulting Leo for help in getting the facts straight was an old habit she should probably try to break, but then again, he was her editor now—for the time being, while Burt was recovering—so why not share her conclusions with him.

When she got Leo's greeting, asking her to leave a message, Vivian almost hung up, but then said, "Leo, it's Vivian. I've been looking at the files on the jump drive. I want you to come over and take a look. The scandal at St. Killian Bank centers around one man, a guy named Grant Stone. He's a vice president at the bank. Not only that, but the evidence on this jump drive shows that Grant Stone is the man who stole Amal's money. Grant Stone is the man Amal came to St. Killian to confront. I think Grant Stone killed Amal."

After ending the call, Vivian paused and took a deep breath, jolted by the words she'd spoken. Verbalizing the name of Amal's murderer made her heart slam and her blood boil. Vivian was positive Grant Stone had run over Amal, leaving her for dead in the parking lot of the Purple Gecko.

Amal's murder wasn't Stone's only crime, though.

The speculation about Grant Stone killing Marlie O'Neal had been spinning like a dervish in her head since she'd begun to make sense of the spreadsheets on the jump drive. Now, the spinning had stopped, and the truth was so obvious. Marlie O'Neal had proof that Grant Stone was a cold-blooded thief, stealing from his customers. When Marlie threatened to expose Stone's crimes, the son of a bitch had strangled her.

Vivian's chest tightened, thinking of Stone. The skeeve. Vice president at St. Killian Bank, the married man Marlie had been sleeping around with. The bastard had to be caught. Vivian wouldn't rest until Stone was tried, convicted, and thrown in jail for what he'd done.

At once, Vivian wanted to find out everything she could about him. Turning to her computer, she accessed the website for St. Killian Bank. Seconds later, she used the site map to find a page called Leadership. There she found the bank's chairman, CEO, and CFO. Under another tab, there was a list of the bank's vice presidents. Vivian found Grant Stone's name and clicked on it.

Staring at Grant Stone's profile page, Vivian's heart thundered.

The stylized professional photo staged to make the bank executive look competent, decisive, and trustworthy, highlighted the banker's features. Vivian's head pounded as realization hit her like a punch in the gut. Shaking her head in disbelief, Vivian whispered, "I know this man …"

Chapter Thirty-Six

Her heart pounding, Vivian scanned Grant Stone's profile.

With over twenty years of banking experience, he oversaw the bank's branch operations, its retail and mortgage lending functions, and call center. In addition, he directed deposit generation activity for the bank.

Struggling to manage her outrage, Vivian jumped up and turned away from the desk, facing the wall of windows overlooking the sprawling, palm-dotted manicured lawns of the plaza.

Trying to catch her breath, Vivian told herself to calm down and focus. She needed to think, so she could figure out what to do, but her mind was in shambles. Grant Stone's face floated into her head. Vivian couldn't believe she knew the skeevy bank vice president. She had talked to the bastard who'd killed both Amal and Marlie O'Neal.

Rage flared within her, bringing tears to her eyes. She had talked to Amal's killer. She had been face to face with the man who had run over her best friend, the man who'd strangled Marlie. A sob escaped, but Vivian willed herself not to cry. She had to keep it together. Somehow, someway. Leo would come soon. He had to have gotten her message by now. When he showed up, Vivian would share the sickening new developments with him, and they would take all the proof they'd gathered to Baxter François.

Once the detective had all the information, he would have no choice but to arrest Grant Stone for murder.

Taking a deep breath, Vivian closed her eyes. Maybe she should call Leo again? And Detective François, she needed to call him, too. Thinking about the jump drive, Vivian realized she should probably make several copies of the evidence against Grant Stone, just in case—

Something thick and hard snaked around her neck. Screaming, terrified and confused, Vivian's eyes opened. A faint reflection in the windows showed a hazy image of someone standing behind her. A man, she could tell, several inches taller, wearing a black mask, the eyes and mouth cut out. His heavy arm tightened around her, sending Vivian's heart into her throat as she clawed at the intruder's arm, digging her nails into his flesh.

"Give me the jump drive, bitch!" The man's hot, fetid breath seemed to burn across her ear and cheek as he pulled her away from the leather chair, dragging her around in front of the desk. Struggling and gasping, Vivian tried to yank away from him.

"I know you got that jump drive!" The man spun her around to face him and then backhanded her across the face. "Give it to me!"

Reeling from his blow, Vivian stumbled back against the desk. The intruder reached for her again, and Vivian ducked from his grasp. Grabbing a crystal paperweight from the desk, she threw it at him, catching him in the mouth, leaving behind a bloody gash across his bottom lip.

"Bitch!" He touched his mouth and stared at his fingers.

Vivian lurched to the right, toward the bookshelves lining the wall. She grabbed a large dictionary and turned. The man was rushing to her. Vivian hurled the dictionary at him, hoping to knock him in the head, maybe cause him to stumble so she could get past him and out of the study.

The intruder blocked the dictionary with his arm, sending it flying away from him, and grabbed her by both arms, shaking her. "Where is that jump drive? Give it to me!"

"Go to hell!" Vivian screamed, kicking him in the shin.

He grunted but didn't drop to his knees, as she'd hoped he would. Leo had taught her several ways to defend herself, but she hadn't had to fight for her life for so long. She couldn't remember what to do.

The intruder slapped her again, harder, and then shoved her back against the bookshelves. The wind knocked from her, Vivian slumped to the floor. Her cheek pressed against the cool hardwood, she thought of escape. How was she going to get away from this bastard? Who the hell was he? Grant Stone? The banker knew she had the jump drive. Had he broken into her home to ransack her condo in his search for the evidence that would put him behind bars?

Out of nowhere, Marlie O'Neal's lifeless body slipped into her mind. Stone had killed Marlie before he'd searched for the jump drive. Was Stone going to kill her too? No, Vivian told herself. No, she wasn't going to die, she couldn't—

Fingers grabbed her braids and yanked, forcing her head back.

Wincing from the pain, Vivian scrambled to get to her knees, desperate to—

A damp cloth smashed into her mouth and nose. An acrid chemical smell spiraled into her nostrils, rendering her light-headed, making her eyes water. *Drugged.* The realization was worse that a punch in the face. The intruder had drugged her. Something on that cloth was making her feel as though—

"Get the hell away from her!"

Abruptly, Vivian felt the fingers in her hair draw back. Released from the intruder's grasp, she dropped to the floor with a thud, banging the back of her skull. A shock wave of pain vibrated through her body as she rolled onto her side. Perplexed, her vision slightly blurred, Vivian pushed up onto her elbow. About four or five feet away, in the center of the study, the intruder was on his knees, trying to escape the headlock he'd been put into.

Vivian blinked again, hazy from the chemicals on the cloth. Was that Leo with his arm around the intruder's throat?

"Who the hell are you?" The voice was Leo's demanding baritone. "How did you get in here?"

The intruder said nothing as he wrestled against Leo and found a way to ram his elbow back into Leo's gut. Grunting, Leo dropped to one knee, and the intruder took advantage, ramming his elbow into Leo again until he was able to slip out of the headlock.

On his feet, the intruder kicked toward Leo, but Leo anticipated the move. Grabbing the intruder's foot, Leo yanked, sending the man crashing to the floor. On him in an instant, Leo grabbed the intruder by the collar of his black T-shirt, yanked him to a sitting position, and slammed his fist into the intruder's jaw. Once, twice, over and over, until the intruder slumped forward, head lolling against his chest.

Woozy and disoriented, Vivian called out for Leo, her voice a hoarse croak as she slipped back to the floor, staring at the ceiling.

"Viv! Vivian!"

Leo's voice sounded as though it was far away, and maybe underwater, Vivian wasn't sure. She was just tired. So very tired. She needed to close her eyes, to sleep for a moment.

"Vivian ..."

A light tap against her cheek forced her eyes open. Leo's face hovered above her, his piercing blue eyes full of fear and concern. "Viv, stay with me, okay? Don't go to sleep. I'm going to call the cops and an ambulance. But, stay awake, Viv. Don't close your eyes."

But, she had to close her eyes, just for a moment.

Chapter Thirty-Seven

"How are you, Ms. Thomas?"

"Okay, I guess." Vivian pushed the button to lift the hospital bed to a sitting position. "Still a little woozy. The doctors wanted to keep me overnight to monitor me."

"I'm not surprised," the detective said. "After all, you did get a nose full of chloroform."

"Wasn't chloroform," Vivian said, recalling what the doctor had told her when he'd stopped by to check on her during his morning rounds. "They're not sure what it was. The doctors said it was some homemade concoction. They're sending it to a lab in Amargo to find out exactly what was on that cloth."

"Amargo? They sent it to the Aerie Islands?"

"They have a new state-of-the-art medical facility that opened last year," Vivian said. "Beanie covered the groundbreaking ceremony. The only hospital in the Caribbean that has a Level 4 research lab, apparently."

The detective frowned. "Yeah, I heard about that."

"Doesn't seem as though you liked what you heard," Vivian remarked, curious about his distracted stare.

Shaking his head, he said, "No, actually, I heard that it's an excellent hospital, but ..."

"But ..."

"Let's talk about the attack on your life, Ms. Thomas," said the detective, squashing the subject. "You up for answering a few questions?"

"Sure," Vivian said.

"I haven't had a chance to talk to Leo Bronson yet, but I was told that he called 9-1-1 to report the attack." The detective pulled a chair closer to the bed and flipped a few pages in his steno pad. "According to the deputy on duty, Mr. Bronson said he showed up at your place and saw the garage door was open. He entered your condo and heard screaming that he determined was coming from upstairs, where he found a masked intruder in the process of attacking you. He then pulled the intruder away from you and went all mixed martial arts on the guy."

"Leo just hit the guy a few times," Vivian said, recalling the moments before she'd blacked out, watching Leo slam his fist into her attacker's face. "He was just trying to get the guy off me."

"He did more than just get the guy off you," said the detective. "He knocked the man unconscious. Very heroic."

Vivian's cheeks grew warm, and she glanced toward the window, away from the detective's sly gaze.

She wasn't sure how she felt about Leo being her hero, but she was thankful he'd shown up when he had. She could have been killed. Definitely, she would have lost the evidence she had against that bastard Grant Stone. The attacker had demanded the jump drive, and with her unconscious, he would have been free to search her study and would have eventually found what he'd broken into her condo to find.

Leo had saved her life. If not for him, there was no telling what would have happened to her. So many times over their five-year relationship, she wouldn't have made it if not for Leo. From the first moment they'd met, she'd known, somehow, that he would be crucial to her life, essential to her existence.

"I don't know how heroic it was," Vivian demurred. "I'd called Leo to come over to discuss some things, so he was just in the right place at the right time to help me. He would have done the same thing for anybody."

The detective's grin was wry. "Sounds like a hero to me."

"So, you came to ask me some questions," Vivian said. "Actually, I'm glad to see you. I need to tell you about the guy who broke into my condo."

Tilting his head, eyes shrewd, he asked, "You know the intruder?"

"I know he was looking for the jump drive," Vivian said. "And that's not the only thing I know."

"What do you mean?"

"Amal Shahin was not the victim of a hit and run," Vivian said, glaring at him. "My best friend was murdered. And I know who killed her."

Chapter Thirty-Eight

"Okay, Ms. Thomas, let's see if I have your story straight."

"It's not a story," Vivian said, irritated. "It's the truth. Grant Stone killed Amal. We can go over the facts again, if you want, as many times as you want, but the truth isn't going to change. Grant Stone murdered Amal. You need to arrest him."

"Ms. Thomas, you are making very serious accusations," the detective said. "Before I can even think of arresting Mr. Stone, I need to make sure there is proof to support your claims."

"It's all on the jump drive," Vivian said, trying not to scream at him. "I told you, Grant Stone broke into my condo because he wanted that jump drive. He didn't want me to show the evidence on the jump drive to the police because he knew it would prove he's a cold-blooded killer."

"Let's talk about the jump drive again," the detective suggested. "Now, first of all, you obtained this jump drive from a woman named Renee Greenwood."

"Right, Renee gave me the jump drive," Vivian said, frustrated by the detective's unnecessary fastidiousness. He was wasting time, going over and over the details of what she had told him. He was looking for holes in her story when he should have been arresting Grant Stone.

"Renee had gotten the jump drive from Marlie who planned to give it to me the day she died."

"That's when you went to her house to meet with her," the detective confirmed.

"I believe Marlie was going to tell me that Grant Stone was stealing from some of his clients."

"One of whom was your friend, Amal Shahin," said the detective.

Vivian nodded. "And I believe Grant Stone was the man who was in Marlie's house that day. He was looking for the jump drive. When I called out to Marlie, Stone must have heard me. He hit me in the head with something so he could get away."

"But, you didn't see Grant Stone in Marlie's house that day," the detective pointed out.

"I know it was him," Vivian insisted. "He went there to get the jump drive from Marlie, but she didn't have it. Remember, I told you Marlie had asked Renee to keep it because Marlie was absent-minded and thought she might lose it before she could give it to me."

"Renee Greenwood gives you the jump drive, but it's password protected," the detective said, glancing at his notes. "You had your colleague's cousin figure out the password for you."

Vivian said, "The jump drive contained about a dozen Excel spreadsheets and one mp4 file. None of the spreadsheets made any sense."

"But, then you checked out the media file," said the detective, consulting his notes. "It was a video of Marlie O'Neal explaining how Grant Stone was stealing from some of his clients."

"At first, I was hesitant to open it," Vivian said, remembering Renee's warning about the jump drive containing porn. "But, if I hadn't watched that video, I wouldn't have found out the truth."

"Let's recap what you allege was on the video," the detective said, a hint of skepticism in his tone.

"You could watch the video yourself," Vivian pointed out. "Didn't Leo give the police the jump drive?"

"He did," the detective confirmed. "But, oblige me, if you don't mind."

For what seemed like the hundredth time, Vivian explained the extent of Grant Stone's crimes:

Before his job at St. Killian Bank, Grant Stone worked at a bank in Grand Cayman. At the Grand Cayman bank, Stone was responsible for all new accounts. Several of those accounts were opened for the purpose of criminal intent, most notably, money laundering. Stone had about two dozen shady clients for whom he provided money laundering services.

Amal had been one of Stone's clients.

Officials at the Grand Cayman bank suspected Stone of laundering money, but before they could fire him, he resigned and moved to St. Killian, where he took a position at St. Killian Bank. However, Stone neglected to tell his criminal clients that he no longer worked at the Grand Cayman bank.

A few of those criminal clients at the Grand Cayman bank had fairly inactive accounts which they used for deposits only.

Before leaving the Grand Cayman bank, Grant changed the addresses on these accounts so criminal clients wouldn't get notifications from the Grand Cayman bank. Stone falsified bank statements and sent those fake bank statements to the criminal clients, making it appear as though their money was still sitting in the Grand Cayman bank.

The truth was, Stone was taking the illegal cash profits from his criminal clients, depositing the cash into the Grand Cayman bank and then transferring the clients' cash from the Grand Cayman bank to his account at St. Killian Bank.

After an exhale, the detective said, "You believe that initially, Marlie planned to give the jump drive to Amal, but when Amal was killed, Marlie decided to give the evidence about Stone's crimes to you."

Vivian said, "The day Amal was murdered, we'd gone to lunch earlier, and someone kept texting Amal. I could tell Amal was pissed, but she told me it was some issue with her company. Later, when we went back to my condo, I overheard her having a very tense, angry conversation, and she said something like I'm going to kill that bastard. Amal told me she was upset about a vendor and just venting her frustration, but I believe she was talking to Marlie O'Neal about how Grant Stone had stolen her money."

"So, you think Marlie was going to give Amal the proof she needed to put Grant Stone behind bars," the detective said. "But you claim Amal wasn't in a position to go to the cops seeing as how she was using her medical spa business as a front to sell prescription drugs. And that's why you believe she bought a gun illegally from Landon George to handle Stone on her own."

"Look, I know Amal wasn't a saint, okay?" Vivian said, conflicted, feeling the need to defend Amal even though she was still angry and disappointed by the disastrous choices her best friend had made. "But, she didn't deserve to be run over."

"No, she didn't," the detective agreed.

"That's why you need to arrest Grant Stone," Vivian said. "He killed Amal, and then he killed Marlie, and he attacked me last night."

"Grant Stone didn't attack you."

Perplexed, Vivian shook her head. "What do you mean?"

"You didn't see the man who broke into your condo," the detective said.

"But, I know it was Grant Stone," Vivian said. "It had to be. Who else wanted that damn jump drive?"

"When the police arrived at your condo last night," said the detective, "the intruder was still unconscious. He was taken to the hospital and placed under police custody. When he finally came to a few hours later, handcuffed to his bed, he was willing to talk if we were willing to convince the prosecutor to plea bargain."

"What did he tell you?"

"The man's name is Waldo Esperance," the detective said, flipping through his steno pad again. "He's from St. Killian, but only just returned eight months ago, after doing a three-year stint at a minimum-security prison in Florida. He's been looking for permanent work, but in the meantime, he does odd jobs for his uncle, Gasper Esperance, who works for a wealthy gentleman that's got a spread out in Marchmont. Waldo claims the wealthy gentleman approached him and offered to pay him to break into your condo and steal the jump drive."

"And this wealthy gentleman is Grant Stone," Vivian said. "What more do you need to arrest that bastard?"

Standing, the detective sighed. "Actually—and this is off the record, by the way—I'm planning to have a talk with Mr. Stone. Yesterday evening, I received some information which leads me to believe that you're right about him being involved in the murder of Marlie O'Neal."

"What kind of information?"

"Information that I don't want to see on the front page of the *Palmchat Gazette*," The detective said, adding a slight smile. "I don't want to tip Stone off, or worse, spook him. He's got the means to disappear very quickly if he has to."

"The *Palmchat Gazette* won't mention anything until after Stone is arrested," Vivian said, hoping the detective would agree to her offer. "And then we'd like an exclusive with you."

Rubbing his chin, his gaze considerate, the detective said, "Not so sure about the exclusive interview, but after Stone is arrested, you can let your readers know that we finally got access to Marlie O'Neal's cell phone and there were several threatening text messages from Grant Stone."

"You have to arrest him," Vivian said, her heart pounding wildly. "He's dangerous, and he is evil."

"Evil?" The detective arched a brow.

Tears pricked her eyes. Turning toward the wide bay window, Vivian swiped her cheeks and then glanced at the detective again. "I know Grant Stone. I talked to him. I questioned him about Amal, and he sat right across from me, and he knew that he had run her over, and he pretended he didn't know who she was ..."

Stepping closer to the bed, the detective took her hand. "What are you talking about? When did you talk to Grant Stone?"

Sniffing, Vivian said, "A few days ago, I went to the Purple Gecko to see if any of the employees had seen Amal in the bar that night. I was wondering if she'd met someone in the bar and maybe left with that person. The bartender didn't remember Amal, but he told me about one of his regular customers, a man named Mr. Jameson."

"What does this Mr. Jameson have to do with Grant Stone?"

Staring at the detective, feeling desolate and like a fool, Vivian said, "Before I was attacked, I looked up Grant Stone on the St. Killian Bank website. As soon as I saw his picture, I knew him. I recognized that silver hair and that strong jaw, like a middle-aged Ken doll. The regular customer at the Purple Gecko made me think his name was Mr. Jameson, but that wasn't true. Mr. Jameson is Grant Stone."

Chapter Thirty-Nine

"Well, Detective," Leo's words pierced the air, "if that isn't enough to get Grant Stone arrested, I don't know what is."

Vivian stared at Leo as he leaned against the doorframe of her hospital room. Coiled muscles and arms crossed tightly over his chest, Leo's annoyance by the detective's presence, nearly three hours after he'd left them, was palpable. His polite tone was in stark contrast to his body language, which was telling Baxter François to get the hell out.

"Mr. Bronson, as I was telling Ms. Thomas, we have gathered enough evidence to seek an arrest warrant for Grant Stone. I will let you both know when we have him in custody," Detective François said. After a quick nod at Vivian, the detective left.

Leo's face relaxed as he walked into the hospital room, closing the door behind him with a gentle push of his foot. As he crossed in front of her bed and plopped down on the worn sienna faux leather chair in the corner, Vivian felt a flutter in her chest. Reflecting on the events from last night, she couldn't deny that Leo had been her hero. More than that, he'd been her protector and her safe place as she dealt with the aftermath of the attack.

She'd woken up in the emergency room with Leo lying next to her in the bed, holding her, against the nurses' and doctor's orders. He'd wanted her to feel safe when she finally woke up from whatever mystery cocktail that was in the cloth the attacker used to knock her out. Through rounds of tests and a cycle of drifting in and out of consciousness, Leo had remained by her side, whispering words in her ear. She was comforted by his words and his presence, even though she couldn't remember exactly what he'd said.

Around two that morning, she'd finally emerged fully awake and noticed Leo dozing. Sitting on a stool next to her bed, Leo was hunched over with his head resting against her stomach. He'd looked adorable sleeping, nostrils flaring softly and his chestnut-brown curls in an unkempt halo around his head. She couldn't resist caressing his face, and he woke immediately from her touch.

Her mind had been racing from the evidence she'd found against Grant Stone, implicating him as the killer of both Marlie and Amal. Though he seemed exhausted, Leo had listened to every angle of evidence Vivian had discovered and agreed with her conclusions. He'd believed her theories and encouraged her to discuss them with Detective François.

As Vivian drifted back to sleep with the sunrise glowing through the window, she knew she'd love Leo forever, this man who managed to be with her through thick and thin during the most critical times in her life. But her love was tainted, bittersweet, because she knew she could never settle for what Leo was willing to give nor would she ever demand more from him.

"What took you so long?" Vivian asked, giving Leo a once-over. He was still wearing the same clothes from last night and apparently hadn't gone home. "I thought you were going to stop by the newspaper to do a quick check on things, not be gone for several hours."

"Well, Ms. Thomas, if I didn't know any better, I'd think that you missed me." A bright smile spread across his face, wattage strong enough to melt her heart.

Vivian folded her arms over her chest, unable to suppress returning his smile. She had missed Leo. He'd been a constant presence with her throughout this ordeal, and she liked having him with her.

"I lost track of time looking through the files on the jump drive," Leo answered.

"How'd you do that?" Vivian asked, sitting up in the bed. "I thought the police took the jump drive last night."

"Stevie's cousin made a copy, of course. Everything was like you said. All signs point to Grant Stone as the man who killed Marlie and stole Amal's money. The cops have more than enough evidence on him for Marlie's murder, but Amal's may be a bit harder."

"It still looks like a classic hit-and-run case." Vivian looked down at her hands, anger tickling across her skin as she thought about the real possibility that the police may not have enough evidence to tie Grant Stone to Amal's murder. "I'm so frustrated and angry. With every piece of evidence we have on that bastard, it's all circumstantial as it relates to Amal's death. He'll get convicted of murdering Marlie and stealing, but I want justice for Amal. I shouldn't care after everything I found out about her, but I do."

"I couldn't care less about getting justice for Amal," Leo muttered, a strange look passing across his face as he stared absently toward a corner of the room.

"What?" Vivian shook her head, not sure what to make of the abrupt change in Leo's demeanor. "I don't understand."

"How can you not understand?" Leo asked, a tinge of anger in his tone. "Grant Stone was so desperate to keep his scam from being exposed that he killed not one but two people. On top of that, he knows you are on to him, and he has attacked you not once, but twice."

Vivian shuddered at Leo's words, recognizing the fear he must be feeling knowing how close she came to the killer.

"Grant Stone knows by now that the thug he hired got arrested and that you've given the jump drive to the police. Do you know what that means?" Leo demanded.

Vivian stilled her body from the onslaught of Leo's words, the truth in his statements she hadn't let herself acknowledge yet.

"Viv, you are this bastard's next target," Leo said, his blue eyes darkening with worry. "I don't want the next message I get to be a call from François telling me you're dead."

Chapter Forty

Vivian wrapped her arms around Leo. Her head pressed against his chest, listening to the frenetic beats of his heart. Instinct had compelled her to comfort him as his voice broke with emotion, sharing the fears that were pent up within him since he found her semi-unconscious last night.

As she held him tighter, Leo's muscles began to relax from the tense strain as he enveloped her in his arms. Seeing the misery in his eyes and hearing the fear in his words had been too much for Vivian. She needed him to know there was no way she'd be Grant Stone's next victim. That bastard had taken too much from her already, and she wasn't going to let him ruin whatever this was that she had with Leo now. They were in a good place. One she didn't quite understand, but she knew it was where she wanted to be. Trying to define this new situation she and Leo coexisted in was exhilarating and frustrating, but she'd learned from him being on the island for the past month that they were meant to be in each other's lives. And she was at peace with her decision to let him back in. The sadness of what could have been between them wasn't enough to stop her from welcoming this reunion.

"I don't want to lose you again," Leo said, words muffled as he whispered them into her hair before placing a gentle kiss on her forehead.

"That's not going to happen. You know I'm too stubborn to die," Vivian said, poking a finger in Leo's side.

He didn't smile. Releasing her from his embrace, Leo led Vivian back to the bed and sat next to her.

"This isn't funny. This is your life we're talking about."

"I know, and I'm not trying to make light of it. I just don't want you to worry."

Reaching into his pocket, Leo pulled out a folded piece of paper. The same folded piece of paper she'd found in the soapstone box on his credenza at the bungalow. The breakup letter she'd written to him almost a year and a half ago when she'd walked out of his life.

Leo held it out toward her.

Vivian resisted taking the paper, no longer wanting any reminder of the end of their relationship. She wanted to be in this moment with Leo, ignoring the past failures and focusing on what was happening here and now.

"When I first got this letter, I was devastated. More than devastated, it broke me," Leo said, letting the letter fall onto the rough cotton blanket of her hospital bed. "I deserve a chance to respond to the things you said in that letter."

Leo paused, desolation etched across his face. Vivian's heart broke all over again, and she regretted ending their relationship with a stupid letter. If she was honest with herself, she probably regretted ending their relationship at all.

Leo continued, "I knew I would find you eventually. I wanted a chance to make things right."

"There's nothing to make right. What we had was beautiful and precious, and it's something that we both will cherish forever. It doesn't matter that it didn't last."

"Yes, it does matter!" Leo erupted. "If you'd just given me a chance, I would have changed for you. I would have done anything to keep you—married you, had babies with you, whatever it took."

"That's not why I wrote the letter. I wasn't trying to give you an ultimatum or manipulate you into doing what I wanted," Vivian retorted, disappointed that Leo thought fixing their relationship would have been that simple. Agreeing to something he didn't believe in would have led to resentment. It would have eroded the love they had cherished and destroyed their relationship slowly. They would still have ended up where they were now, having endured more time of suffering to get there. Maybe ending things quickly had been for the best.

"I know that now," Leo said, grabbing both of her hands in his.

Vivian felt her body tremor from his touch, not believing the words he uttered.

"When I couldn't find you, it forced me to look within myself and understand how everything had fallen apart. I realized that it wasn't about me giving in. You just needed me to respect the relationship we'd built, the unconditional love we have for each other. It took being away from you for over a year to realize the importance of marriage."

Tears began to slide down Vivian's cheeks.

"I was scared to death of losing you. Everything I thought would keep us together was exactly what tore us apart." Leo shook his head as if trying to shake away the memories of his old perspectives on relationships and marriage. "But love always protects, always trusts, always hopes, and always perseveres. There is no fear in love."

A pure honesty and earnestness lingered in Leo's words, a testament to the veracity of his journey and the agony that led to his understanding. His recognition, finally, of her feelings and her views was a welcomed and beautiful gift.

"You never had a chance, Leo. Burt told me how screwed up he was after his divorce from your mom. How he'd been reckless, disparaging marriage and warning you against it. I understand why you fought against getting married now," Vivian said.

"I was never against marriage; I was just against losing you. I honestly believed that what happened to my parents would be our destiny. I should never have hung on to those crazy beliefs for so long, not after I'd grown up and was smart enough to know better." Leo grinned and winked at her. "When you left, I grew up real fast. Because of that I really learned what love truly is and what an honor and a privilege it is to marry the one woman you love more than life itself."

Vivian felt her heart thumping in her chest.

"You really still love me?" Vivian asked, tentative with her words, bewildered by the unexpectedness of this moment with Leo.

"I never ever stopped. I have loved you from the moment I first laid eyes on you, standing on the deck of that boat in the middle of Lake Nassar. I will love you and protect you and honor you and, if you still want it, commit to being with you forever as your husband."

Vivian dropped her head in her hands. What was happening? Had Leo really changed his mind about marriage? Could he really have overcome his distrust? She'd never imagined that he would ever change his views, yet here he was pouring his heart out to her, telling her everything she'd longed to hear.

"It was no coincidence that I found you at the street carnival. Fate brought us together at the right moment. After we made love and you ran off," Leo said, letting out a slight chuckle, "I wasn't even upset. I thought to myself, there goes my future wife."

"Your wife!" Vivian said, eyes wide. "Are you serious?"

The look on Leo's face left no doubt in his answer.

"I came back here for you."

"You came back for Burt, to help him with the paper."

"My dad didn't need me to run this paper. There are dozens of more experienced editors he could have flown in from any of his other papers to do that job easily," Leo said, leaning toward her. "He knew I needed to be with you, and that's why he offered the job to me. And I took it."

Vivian was stunned.

"So, I flew back to New York and took a leave of absence from The Times. While I was there, I took a stroll through the Diamond District and bought this …"

Leo held open his hand, and lying against his palm was a single emerald cut diamond, the size of a dime, set in a platinum eternity band of smaller round diamonds.

Vivian gasped, her hands flying to her mouth as the sunlight danced against the stone, creating sparkles.

"But, you can't have it yet." Leo laughed as he placed the ring on his pinky and twirled it around. "I know it won't be that easy for us to get back together. I'm just asking you to give us another chance. I love you more now than ever before. You make me a better man, Vivian Thomas. Can we try this again?"

Dizzy from Leo's metamorphosis, Vivian leaned back and closed her eyes. She wanted to pinch herself, not trusting that the last hour with him had happened. Could they rebuild their relationship and make it stronger and better than before? Or had too much time passed? Perhaps they were too different now, scathed from the memories and wouldn't be able to rekindle the passionate love they'd shared for five years.

Confused and mortified, Vivian struggled to respond, opening her mouth and then closing it again as she tried to figure out how to answer Leo's question.

After several moments of contemplation, she looked into Leo's hopeful eyes and said, "I need to think about it."

Chapter Forty-One

Vivian buckled her seat belt, started the Range Rover, and then backed out of the parking space in the *Palmchat Gazette* parking lot.

Moments ago, Caleb had told her about something interesting he'd heard on the police scanner he'd been monitoring—a dead body found in the jungle on the east side of the island. Deciding the situation might develop into a story, Vivian had taken the information and headed out of the *Palmchat Gazette* office, grateful to get away from her desk, where she'd been half-heartedly fact checking one of her articles.

Turning onto the main road, Vivian stared through the windshield, noticing several low thunderheads, dark and ominous, scuttling across the sky from the west. Thunderstorms had been threatening all morning, and it looked as though they were about to make good on their promise.

Vivian didn't mind.

The rain and wind would chase away the stifling humidity that had gripped the island for the past week. The oppressive heat had been an irritant, adding to her frustration with the St. Killian Police Department. Four days had passed since Vivian had been attacked by the thug Grant Stone had hired to break into her condo and steal the jump drive. Despite the compelling evidence she'd given Detective François, and the detective's own vow to question Stone about the murder of Marlie O'Neal, the homicidal banker had yet to be interrogated by the police.

According to her sources at the station, the St. Killian police hadn't yet been able to locate Stone, which Vivian didn't understand. The man worked at St. Killian bank and had a mansion in Marchmont. How hard could it be to find him?

Unfortunately, very hard, Vivian knew. A man of considerable means like Stone would have no problem disappearing, especially if he believed his crimes were quickly catching up with him. Vivian prayed Stone hadn't already left the island, but she feared he might be long gone.

Glancing at Caleb's directions, written on a sticky note she'd pressed against the cubby hole, Vivian turned off onto a paved two-lane street cut between thick, dense rain forest. As she drove farther east, the tropical vegetation grew more lush and thick. East St. Killian was sparsely populated, and while not as economically stable as the rest of the island, it still benefited from its reputation as a hiker's paradise.

As the road twisted and curved, Vivian's thoughts shifted to the confusing conundrum with Leo.

Since the last time she and Leo had discussed their complicated situation, Vivian had tried to make good on the promise she'd made him to think about how she would answer his question.

"Can we try this again?"

But how could she come to a rational and logical conclusion when she was still trying to recover from the shock of the engagement ring he'd bought her.

"I took a stroll through the Diamond District and bought this ..."

The diamond was gorgeous, the perfect ring given to her by the perfect man, who knew emerald cut was her favorite diamond shape.

Vivian didn't know if she should be elated or insulted. On the one hand, what she wanted most in the world was to be Leo's wife. She wanted to accept the ring and tell him yes, she would marry him. And yet, she couldn't forget the pain she'd endured when he'd broken her heart. The desolation and despair could have been avoided if he had been self-aware and sensitive enough to realize his views on marriage had been tainted by two people who should have never entered into holy matrimony in the first place.

Vivian exhaled as the windshield wipers automatically came on, sensing the first few drops of rain.

Despite the chasm their differences had created between them, they had never stopped loving each other. But she wondered, was it finally time for them to cross the divide? Was it time to put the past behind them? Vivian had never stopped believing they belonged together. He was the love of her life; she was the only woman he wanted. They were soul mates.

Not many people got a second chance at love. Should she embrace the blessing and give Leo the answer he wanted?

"Can we try this again?"

She still wasn't sure.

Steering out of a tricky N-curve, Vivian saw several police cars about fifty feet ahead on the straightaway, blocking the road, lights flickering in a kaleidoscope of red and blue, illuminating the trees.

Two cops stood in the middle of the street, directing traffic. One of the officers stopped southbound traffic while another deputy directed cars around the vehicles obstructing the northbound lane. Steering the Range Rover onto the shoulder, Vivian parked about ten feet behind the last cop car, as close as possible to the trees, mindful of the ditch. Cutting the engine, she grabbed her cross-body purse and her cell phone and then exited the SUV.

Outside the air was thick and humid, sharp with the smell of a storm. In the distance, she heard the rumbling of thunder, and as she approached one of the policemen, fat raindrops hit her lashes and the tip of her nose.

During a break in the traffic, Vivian approached one of the cops, a young deputy she'd interviewed before, and showed him her press credentials.

"What's going on?" Vivian asked, zipping up her lightweight rain jacket. "We heard something about a dead body?"

"Backpackers found the body about an hour ago," he said. "Homeless guy. May have overdosed. Coroner is down there with Detective François and a few crime scene techs."

"Mind if I take a look?"

The deputy shrugged. "Be careful going down, though. It's a steep slope."

Thanking the deputy for the heads-up, Vivian pulled the hood of her jacket over her head and angled toward the shoulder. Holding onto branches and limbs, Vivian started down the uneven slope, a natural stairway of hard dirt and horizontal tree trunks strewn with fat, flat elephant leaves. Careful of the slippery, lichen-covered rocks, she continued. Turning sideways, leading with her right foot, she negotiated several large boulders, inching along, breathing hard and damp with sweat. By the time she reached the forest floor, the rain was falling in a steady stream, and the sky had darkened into dusk, even though it was only around five o'clock.

Through a dense copse of neglected banana trees, she spotted several figures milling about. The detective and the crime scene crew, she figured, making her way through the banana trees. The techs appeared to be methodically circling what looked like a small compact car. Weather-beaten and strewn with fallen leaves, it was sun faded, but she could tell the car had been orange. Vivian paused, watching as one of the techs kneeled next to a tire while another climbed into the backseat. Something about the car seemed familiar to her, but she wasn't sure what.

Clustered in a small clearing, she spotted Detective François talking to a deputy and two other people, a man and a woman huddled together, dressed in shorts, T-shirts, and hiking boots. As Vivian came closer, she noticed the couple's pale faces and wide, shell-shocked gazes. The backpackers who'd found the body, Vivian surmised, recalling what the deputy had told her. Inching even closer, Vivian stopped next to a tree, listening as the hikers recounted their tale.

Vivian took out her phone to take notes, jotting down a few details. The couple alternated telling the story, with one of them picking up when the other trailed off, in a sort of tag team fashion. They were adventurous, off-the-beaten-path hikers, hoping to find a trail of their own, one that wasn't offered by one of the St. Killian tour groups or advertised in the guidebooks.

After discovering the path, they'd happened upon an abandoned banana plantation and had decided to explore the surrounding forest. Armed with mosquito repellant, energy bars, water, and a satellite phone, they'd forged ahead.

About an hour into their exploration, they'd come across the abandoned car—and the dead, decomposed body in the passenger's seat.

A moment or two later, Detective François was nodding when he glanced in her direction. Catching his eye, Vivian gave him a wave. He returned her greeting with a frown and then excused himself from the hikers and walked over to her.

"What are you doing here, Ms. Thomas?" he demanded.

"Working the story," she said. "I'd like to talk to those hikers who found the dead body when you're finished grilling them, and it would be nice if you could give me a comment, as well."

"Shouldn't you still be in the hospital?" Detective François pursed his lips, his gaze disapproving. "Last time I checked, the doctors still hadn't gotten the results of whatever was on the rag that your attacker tried to drug you with."

"Relax, Detective," she said. "I feel much better. No headaches, no nausea, no concussion."

Detective François exhaled. "I've finished questioning the hikers. Be my guest."

"Wait a minute," she said, stopping him from walking away.

"Forget about the hikers for a moment. What about Grant Stone? Have you found him yet?"

Pinching the bridge of his nose, the detective said, "We're off the record, Ms. Thomas."

Vivian nodded, noticing that the rain didn't seem to bother the detective. "Fine, whatever."

"We went out to his place and talked to his wife, Georgia," said the detective. "She claims that he's on a business trip in London. Meanwhile, the HR director at St. Killian Bank says Stone is on vacation."

Vivian's stomach dropped. "He's gone, isn't he? He's fled the island. I knew he was going to leave. He's going to get away with killing Amal and Marlie."

"Not if I can help it," the detective said, confident and determined. "We've got an APB out for him across the Palmchat Islands. He's not going to get away with murder. I promise you."

Vivian looked away, wishing she could believe him. She wanted to be hopeful and positive, wanted to believe good would triumph over evil, but she'd seen too many atrocities and too much corruption.

"I hope you're not worrying about Stone coming after you," the detective said.

"No, I'm not," Vivian said. "I'm very thankful for the deputy you assigned to watch out for me."

Since Leo was in the Aerie Islands meeting with the owner of the *Aerie Observer*, who was thinking of selling the publication, the St. Killian Police Department had a cop patrolling the immediate area around her condo.

"Officer Rambla is a good cop," the detective said. "He'll make sure nothing bad—"

"Detective François ..." someone called out.

Startled, Vivian glanced left. A tall, gaunt deputy rushed toward them, his baby face betraying a worried excitement. Seconds later, he reached them, slightly out of breath, squinting from the raindrops.

Detective François asked, "What is it, Officer Tomber?"

"I got the results of the VIN number search for the car that the dead guy was found in," the deputy said. "It's an orange late-model Toyota Corolla belonging to Grant Stone."

Chapter Forty-Two

"The weather is getting worse," Vivian told Deputy Hector Rambla as she stood in the doorway of her garage, which opened to the courtyard. The squat officer was almost as wide as he was tall. The waterproofed parka was too long for his short stature, skimming against the water pooling on the courtyard floor.

"I'm glad you got in before the storm hit," Hector replied. Vivian felt sorry for the guy. Being assigned to babysitting duty as her guard was probably not what he expected when he moved from Mafra, Portugal to St. Killian hoping to fast track his law enforcement career to detective.

"How bad do you think it's going to be?" Hector asked as he hunched slightly, grabbing the edges of his parka down further over his face.

Vivian stared at the increasingly darkening sky. The light patter from earlier in the day was now a steady downpour.

"Thunder and lightning, maybe some wind," she responded. "Street flooding will be the biggest threat, but we're not about to have a hurricane, so don't worry."

"Thank God," Hector said, relief evident in his eyes. "I've never been through a hurricane before."

Vivian took a step back, retreating slightly into the garage away from the plopping rain outside.

"It's no joke, trust me," Vivian said, remembering the category one storm she and Leo had suffered through in Cape Verde off the coast of West Africa a few years ago. The ferocious winds of the storm had been no match for the misery of living without power for two weeks after the storm had passed.

"I'm glad to dodge that bullet," the deputy said, glancing back toward his unmarked police car. It was barely visible from the courtyard, slightly hidden near a palm tree, but it was a perfect location for him to watch her condo for an intruder. Not just any intruder, though. He was watching for Grant Stone.

The deputy lingered, and Vivian could tell he was still a bit uncomfortable with the storm.

"Well, thankfully, St. Killian hasn't been hit by a hurricane in years. All of this will be over by morning," Vivian said, trying to reassure him.

"I hope so. Well, you have a good night, Ms. Thomas," Hector said and turned to walk back to his stakeout vehicle. Vivian watched until he entered the car, before closing the door. Walking through the garage, she entered the back door to her kitchen.

Vivian grabbed a bottle of Felipe beer from the fridge and took a swig, hoping the malted hops would calm her racing mind. She'd never expected the dead body in the jungle to be related in any way to Amal's hit and run. If it hadn't been for the overdose of a homeless drug addict, whose body was discovered by some adventure hikers, the cops never would have found the vehicle. Stone had probably thought the abandoned banana plantation was the perfect hiding place. He had obviously never suspected the Toyota would be found because he hadn't bothered to get rid of the evidence of his crime.

Off the record, as usual, Detective François had told her that the crime scene techs had found traces of blood and skin on the shattered windshield. Inside the vehicle, they'd found fingerprints on the steering wheel, which Vivian prayed would be a match for Grant Stone.

The cops had to find that bastard. Too much time had passed, and with the access he had to millions of dollars of crime money, he could easily be on the other side of the world by now.

Damn it! Hopes fleeting, Vivian tried to relax and trust that Detective François and his deputies would be able to figure out where Grant Stone had fled.

Grabbing her cell phone, Vivian went upstairs to her study and settled into the large leather chair. Typing in the password on her laptop, she decided to get a jump on writing the article on the dead body in the jungle.

Glancing over at her cell phone, she noticed a missed call and a voice message.

Both were from Leo.

A jolt of excitement shot through her body at the thought of him. Leo had kept his promise to give her space to think about her response to his question.

"I'm just asking you to give us another chance."

"Can we try this again?"

Since he'd left for the Aerie Islands a few days ago, Leo hadn't tried to contact her at all, relaying any messages about work for her through Beanie or Caleb.

Vivian wondered why he was calling now. Was he back in St. Killian? More importantly, was she ready to tell him she'd made a decision about their future?

Accessing her voice mail, Vivian put the phone on speaker and heard Leo's baritone fill the study.

"Hey Viv, it's Leo. Just wanted to let you know I'm at the airport. My flight leaves at six, and I should be back home around seven tonight. I hear the weather is worse in St. Killian than here, but the flight isn't delayed. I hope we can continue our conversation when I get back. I love you, Viv."

Vivian pressed her head against her palm. Now that she'd made her decision, she didn't want to delay talking to Leo. They needed to talk tonight. Glancing at the clock, she saw it was almost five.

She had time to call Leo before his plane took off.

Chapter Forty-Three

"Leo ..." Vivian said, sighing. "This is not going to work ..."

"Viv ... just ... call ..." Leo's voice was still breaking up, going in and out. For the past fifteen minutes, Vivian had been trying to talk to him, but the cell reception was atrocious. All she wanted was for him to come over after his plane landed so she could tell him her answer. But, his phone had cut out four or five times as the storm became more intense over the Aerie Islands.

A conversation was pointless during this torrential rain. She should have just waited to call him after seven when he was back on the island. She lived close to the airport, and it would have been easy enough to ask him to stop by after he landed.

Frustrated with the static, Vivian tried once more. "Leo, listen. This isn't working. Call me when your plane lands."

"... wait ... Viv, I ..."

The line went dead again.

Slamming the phone down on the desk, Vivian tried to calm her nerves. It wasn't so bad. Leo would be back in St. Killian in about two hours, and she could try calling him again. She was anxious and nervous about the conversation. In reality, it didn't matter if they talked tonight or in the morning. She had a good idea how the conversation would play out.

Pushing Leo from her mind, Vivian stared at the blank laptop screen. The words for her article hadn't magically appeared. What a time to have writer's block. She forced out a few sentences before giving up. The wind had picked up, and the rain was coming down harder.

Her energy levels were low from the thoughts of Grant Stone, Amal, and Leo coursing through her mind. She really needed to eat. That would help her focus, and maybe she could crank out the article after she got nourishment.

Vivian headed downstairs to the kitchen and made a jerk goat sandwich. Leaning over on the bar, she took a bite. The winds were howling now, and she wondered how Deputy Hector was holding up in his car. Maybe she should invite him inside for safety.

Blackness surrounded her like a cloak without warning.

Dropping her sandwich onto the counter, Vivian fumbled around the kitchen, unable to see her hands in front of her face. The last thing she needed was to be without power. Hopefully, the lights would come back on soon. Vivian struggled to remember where she'd stashed her candles. She thought there should be one in the kitchen, but she couldn't remember. Running her hands along the kitchen cabinets, Vivian opened a few of them and poked around, grabbing handles of pots and pans and a few glasses but no candles.

She remembered she had a large flashlight in the garage. Walking gingerly toward the back of the kitchen, Vivian opened the door and stepped into the garage. Peering into the darkness, she took a few tentative steps, feeling her way along the wall toward the utility shelf. Shuffling slowly, Vivian felt the bumper of her Range Rover. She placed a hand on the SUV to steady herself. The last thing she needed was to do something stupid like sprain an ankle in the darkness.

Vivian took a few more steps, sliding her hands along until she felt the edge of the utility shelf, which ran along half the length of the back wall of the garage. Locating the flashlight, she caught a glimpse of light coming from the door leading to the courtyard.

The door was ajar.

Vivian remembered clearly closing the door earlier after talking to Hector.

Why was it open now?

Her heart began to pound, rattling her rib cage.

Was someone in the garage?

It was nearly impossible to swallow her fear, so she didn't even try as she took one step forward and then another, toward the open door. Vivian could see a sliver of a hibiscus bush, jerking erratically in the wind through the opening.

A shuddering chill passed through her.

Vivian stepped to the door and pushed it open. Outside, rain pelted the bushes and bistro tables in the courtyard. Several of the chairs were overturned as the wind whipped at the potted hibiscus plants.

"Hello?" Vivian called out, her voice snatched away by wind that whipped her braids into a frenzy, back and forth around her shoulders. "Is someone out here?"

Stepping onto the pea gravel, Vivian peered toward the little bistro table near the back of the courtyard.

Someone was lying on the ground next to one of the chairs.

"Oh my God ..." Vivian ran to the person but then slowed, skidding to a stumbling stop.

It was Deputy Hector Rambla.

Vivian's hands began to shake as she saw the blood trailing down the side of his face from the gaping gunshot wound between his eyes.

Chapter Forty-Four

As the rain and wind lashed around her, Vivian stared at the deputy, confused and horrified. Why had someone shot him? What was happening?

Shivering, Vivian dashed back into the garage. She needed to call the police. She needed to tell them Deputy Rambla had been killed. It didn't make sense. Who could have shot him?

Grant Stone's face invaded her mind.

Vivian's heart slammed. Had Grant Stone killed the officer? But, that didn't make sense, did it? Stone couldn't still be on the island, could he? Detective François had told her they hadn't been able to find Stone. His wife thought he was on a business trip and his co-workers thought he was on vacation. Either way, those closest to Stone were under the impression that he wasn't in St. Killian. Vivian believed the same. The bastard had to know the cops were on to him. Why would he stay on the island?

"Viv, you are this bastard's next target."

Exhaling a shaky breath, Vivian hurried back into the house, the flashlight leading the way. In the kitchen, she grabbed the cordless phone. It was dead. *Shit! Where is my cell phone?* Upstairs in the study, she remembered.

Vivian dashed up the stairs and into the den. Lightning flashed like crazy. It wasn't hard to see, even though it was dim. She was turning toward the study when an intense, humid gust swept past her, lifting her braids from her shoulders. Curious and apprehensive, Vivian glanced toward the terrace.

Perplexed, she shined the light toward an object near the couch. Walking toward it, she realized what it was—an outdoor pillow from one of the chaise lounges.

What was the pillow doing inside the den?

Lightning flashed again. Vivian gasped. One of the pocket doors was open. Her heart sped up. Another arc of lightning illuminated the terrace.

A man stood outside the glass panes.

Screaming, Vivian dropped the flashlight. "Oh my God!" Her heart slamming, she stared toward the terrace. Was she seeing things? Had she really seen someone outside?

Afraid to move, she squinted, but it was too dark to make out the shapes. Seconds later, there was another round of lightning. Quickly, she scanned the terrace, but no one was out there. Spooked, she bent down and grabbed the flashlight. Cautiously, she made her way around the furniture, heading for the pocket doors.

After making sure they were locked, she cupped her hands on the glass and peered out at the dark terrace. Wind had blown a few cushions from the chaise lounges, but other than that, there was nothing out there. She must have been seeing things.

Vivian took a breath and turned. With the flashlight cutting through the darkness with a golden glow, Vivian headed between the couches and around a few chairs. She passed the stairwell and went on into the main hallway, which bisected the second floor. Slow and cautious, entering the study, she hurried to the desk where she'd left her cell phone. Vivian set the flashlight on the desk, allowing the cone of light to shine up toward the ceiling. Heading around her desk, she pulled out the leather chair and sat. She glanced around the computer, looking for the cell phone. Where was it? Panic increasing, she pulled out the drawer, wondering if—

Blackness enveloped the room.

Vivian gasped, her pulse roaring through her veins. What had happened to the flashlight? Had the battery died?

Seconds later, lightning illuminated the room, brightening it.

On the opposite side of the desk, a man stood, glaring at her.

Grant Stone.

Chapter Forty-Five

Vivian screamed.

Seconds later, the room was dark again. The lightning subsided as quickly as it had come, plunging the room into darkness where shapes and outlines were still barely visible.

Vivian stood still, terrified, trying to think, to breathe.

Another sizzling light show lit up the study like the Fourth of July.

The deranged banker was gone, no longer on the other side of the desk.

Thunder crashed, like boulders breaking, and the condo shook from the sound vibrations as the hazy darkness claimed the room again. Trembling, Vivian tried not to give in to the terror and despair threatening to do her in. She had been in worse situations, and she had always managed to escape, to stay alive. The banker was a coward. He wasn't a ruthless tribal leader or diabolical foot soldier with allegiance to some megalomaniac dictator. But he was a murderer. He had run Amal over in cold blood. He'd strangled Marlie O'Neal. He was capable of despicable acts.

Darkness shrouded the study as the last round of lightning ended.

Shivering, Vivian tried to wrap her mind around the horror of Stone in her house. Shaking and distraught, she took several deep breaths, trying not to panic. So many times, in the Sudan, she'd followed the trail of bloodthirsty warlords, hacking her way through thick jungle and treacherous terrain in the dead of night, and she'd survived. She could survive a dark study during a thunderstorm with a crazy banker trying to kill her, couldn't she?

Determined not to cry, fighting the fear threatening to overwhelm her, Vivian squinted as she glanced through the darkness, slowly able to discern shapes. Where the hell was Stone? Vivian forced herself to stand still and listen for the imperceptible sounds of breathing or the whisper of footsteps or—

Something cold and flat pressed along the hollow of her throat as an arm snaked across her chest, crushing her. Swallowing, Vivian tried to remember the evasive maneuvers Leo had taught her. He'd shown her how to escape a knife attack, and she'd employed his instructions before, in the Sudan. She'd gotten away from men much more dangerous than Stone, but her mind was blank. She was frozen, terrified of the blade pricking her skin.

She couldn't just stand there and let him cut her throat. She had to do something; she had to—

Abruptly, Vivian felt the arm across her chest move to her neck. With her throat in the crook of the banker's elbow, she gagged, panicked. Scratching and pulling at his forearm, she struggled to stop him from choking her to death. Confused and disoriented, she fought to keep her balance, stumbling as the banker dragged her backward. Digging her heels into the hardwood, she tried to stop his progress, but she started to feel as though she was floating. She was sleepy. Tired of fighting. Tired of struggling. She just wanted to close her eyes for a moment.

There was no time to sleep, she knew. Something within her

screamed at her to stay awake, but she couldn't open her eyes. She couldn't hear anything, couldn't discern the presence of her own body within the darkness. Was she dying, Vivian wondered, as a void of nothingness enveloped her.

Chapter Forty-Six

Vivian's eyes opened and then closed.

A sickening thickness moved through her head, making its way through her veins. In the distance, she heard something like a blast, and all around her was the sound of fine sand against glass. Where was she? What was happening? Was she dreaming?

Determined, Vivian forced one eye open. Through blurred vision, she saw several of her long braids lying across her lap, like black snakes across her tan legs. On top of her braids, her hands were crossed … and bound.

The fog in her head lifted, ushering in a mind-numbing clarity.

Grant Stone was the reason she was tied up. He'd tried to kill her. He'd tried to strangle her, she remembered, but she hadn't died. She must have passed out, and then he'd tied her wrists together, and now …

Where was she now? Vivian kept her head lolled to the side, her chin against her right shoulder and swept her gaze from side to side. She saw oranges stacked in a shallow wicker bowl, and realization dawned. She was in her kitchen, and the lights were back on. Cutting her gaze right, she saw the refrigerator and the rain drumming against the window above the sink.

Keeping her head still, Vivian looked up, taking in the door leading out to the garage. Her heart racing, she narrowed her eyes, glanced left, and saw—

Thunder crashed, startling Vivian, and she jumped, gasping involuntarily. Immediately, she winced at her slip, hoping the banker hadn't heard her.

"I was wondering when you would wake up," said Grant Stone, dashing her hopes. Still, Vivian didn't move and kept her head down, chin on her chest.

Fingers slapped her cheek.

"Don't pretend to be asleep, bitch," the banker warned. "I know you came to."

Jerking her body upright, Vivian turned her head to glare at him.

"Enjoy your nap?" Stone asked, dark eyes glaring as he pulled out the chair across from her and sat. "Hope you got some good rest, but if you didn't, don't worry. You know how people say you can sleep when you're dead? Well, get ready for your final forty winks."

Vivian's pulse jumped. Panic flooded her, and she struggled to breathe, trying not to scream, praying she wouldn't cry. She couldn't lapse into hysteria, couldn't unravel. She had to keep her wits if she planned to get away alive.

"Well, aren't you going to say it? Aren't you going to tell me how I'm not going to get away with this?"

Ignoring the banker, Vivian twisted her wrists beneath the table, trying to free herself from what seemed to be gray electrical tape.

"Well, I am going to get away with this. I have to get away with this. I have no choice."

"What does that mean?" Vivian decided to ask, gritting her

teeth, trying to ignore the pain of the sticky tape rubbing against her flesh.

"No way in hell I'm going to jail, not over that shady bitch Amal."

"Shady?" Vivian asked, enraged by his hypocritical judgment. "That's kind of the pot calling the kettle black, don't you think?"

"Amal was not a good person, okay," said the banker. "She was a drug dealer, you know that? She sold illegal prescription medication to rich women who didn't need it."

"I don't believe you," Vivian said, feigning ignorance, knowing she would have to keep him talking if there was any way she would get out alive.

"The medical spa business wasn't as lucrative as Amal hoped it would be." Stone jumped up and began pacing across the kitchen, from the sink to the stovetop and back again. "She was successful, but she was barely above water, what with all the high-dollar surgeons and massage therapists she had working for her. The best in the business doesn't come cheap, and they wanted to be appropriately compensated. Sometimes, it cost a lot to pay her staff, and she pretty much broke even. Of course, Amal didn't want just to break even. She wanted to be just as rich and glamorous as the women who came to her spa. Problem was, she wanted all that success and glory overnight.

"That's not true," Vivian said. "Amal worked hard to be successful. She was devoted to her company. She wouldn't have risked everything to sell drugs."

Stone laughed out loud. "You really didn't know anything about her, did you?"

"How did you meet Amal?" Vivian asked. Not only did the journalist in her want a complete story, but sending the banker down memory lane might buy her the time she needed to escape her restraints.

"Actually, it was during one of my business trips to Palm Beach," Stone said, returning to the table, standing behind the chair. "My wife had insisted on going with me because she wanted to get some treatments done at a medical spa called Phoenix. A friend of hers had been there and raved about the Botox and the fillers, so of course, my wife, who is vain, delusional, and obsessed with youth, wanted to go. As it turned out, both my wife and I received treatments. My wife got her Botox, and I got Amal."

"What do you mean, you got Amal?" Vivian asked, still trying to loosen the restraints.

"I mean I banged her while my wife was allowing some quack to shoot poison into her forehead," he said, shaking his head. "Best sex I ever had. Dirty and nasty. Addictive. Better than drugs or liquor."

"So you cheated on your wife with Amal?" Vivian asked, drawing on her journalistic training, trying not to think how crazy it was, having a conversation with a cold-blooded murderer.

Stone laughed again. "Quite often. With pleasure. Back then, I made frequent trips to Palm Beach. My wife had developed her own addictions. Botox and Oxycontin. She got her procedures and her illegal prescription medication from Phoenix."

"You expect me to believe that Amal sold drugs to your wife?" Vivian stared at him.

"Here's what you need to understand: Drugs are not a problem exclusive to the poor or the inner city urban jungles," he said, his tone editorializing, as though he was about to give a dissertation. "Rich, privileged women like to bliss out, too. Only, they're not going to stick a needle in their arm or light up a pipe. And they're not going to meet some thug in a back alley after midnight. But, what they will do is buy a three-week supply of Vicodin or Percocet or some other pain-reduction medicine that their regular doctors would be reluctant to prescribe for them, especially if they really didn't need the meds, which most of them don't. Amal knew this, and she took advantage of the opportunity to offer her customers prescription medications without having a valid prescription from a doctor. And, of course, that made her, under federal law, a drug dealer."

Vivian stared at her hands, not sure what to think or how to feel. It was hard to reconcile the Amal she'd thought she'd known with the person Amal had really been.

"When I found out that Amal didn't have a competent laundry service, I told her I would help her out so she wouldn't get busted by some joint task force between the IRS and DEA," he went on. "It was a good partnership."

Curious, Vivian asked, "If the partnership was so good, then why did you start stealing from Amal?"

"I didn't want to steal from Amal," he said, his voice holding a hint of remorse. "I didn't think I would have to. We had a good partnership, and as I said, the sex was fantastic. But then I lost my job at the bank in the Caymans and was forced to take a position at St. Killian Bank. The money wasn't the same, wasn't good enough. St. Killian is expensive, and my wife is accustomed to living in a certain manner, so ..."

"So, you stole from Amal to finance your lavish lifestyle," Vivian said.

"Am I proud of what I did? No, I'm not," he said. "But, I love my wife, and I want her to be happy. She's a very demanding woman. She wants the best and nothing less. I had no choice."

"And I suppose you had no choice but to kill Amal?" Vivian asked, voice quivering with indignation, her heart breaking all over again, thinking of how Amal had suffered. "You were forced to run her down with your car and—"

"I didn't want to kill Amal!" Stone exploded, resuming his frantic pacing. "I was perfectly happy being her partner and lover, but then I made the mistake of getting involved with that dumb bitch Marlie O'Neal."

"Another one of your lovers that you had to kill?"

Stone stopped abruptly and faced her. "Marlie and I had some good times. Most of those times occurred when I would fly to the Caymans to drop off money that my clients wanted me to deposit."

"Your shady, criminal clients that you launder money for, you mean?"

Shrugging, Stone said, "I don't judge. I just provide a much-needed service. It's business."

"You made it personal when you killed Marlie," Vivian said.

"That was actually business, as well," Stone said. "But, Marlie didn't understand that. Marlie was young, silly. She thought she was in love with me, and she wanted me to be in love with her. Crazy bitch wanted me to leave my wife for her. I wasn't about to do that. I'd already done a lot for Marlie, much more than I ever did for any of my other girlfriends."

"Your other girlfriends?" Vivian shook her head, disgusted.

"I bought Marlie that house that you came to meet her at that day."

"The day you killed her," Vivian said. "The day you almost killed me."

"Marlie didn't have to die," Stone said, walking back to the table. "All she had to do was keep her stupid mouth shut. But she was vengeful and vindictive. I didn't want to marry her and live happily ever after, so she tells me that she's going to ruin my life. Crazy bitch tells me that she knows all about the money launder-ing, and she's going to tell my clients that I'm skimming, stealing cash from them. I asked her, are you trying to get me killed? She tells me that she's letting me know that I can't break her heart and get away with it. She tells me she has a jump drive that has evidence on it that could put me in jail."

"So, you went to her house to get the jump drive," Vivian said. "Marlie wouldn't give it to you, so you killed her."

"Again, I didn't want to kill Marlie," Stone insisted. "She would be alive if she had just given me that damn jump drive."

"And Amal would be alive if she had just ... what?"

"Believe it or not, and I'm sure you don't, but I am sorry about Amal," the banker said.

Vivian squeezed her eyes shut, but the tears came anyway, rolling down her face. Minutes passed as the silence stretched, and Vivian worked on loosening the restraints, holding back her urge to sob.

"And I'm sorry that I have to kill you, too," Stone said. "But you know too much, and I can't have you testifying against me, so ..."

"But the police have the jump drive. It has the evidence against you." Adrenaline shooting through her veins, Vivian twisted her wrists. The restraints were starting to loosen, to give a little. She couldn't give up.

"I'm sure a very good attorney could get a judge to rule that the jump drive is inadmissible as evidence," Stone said. "After all, my defense is that Marlie made it all up. She faked the spreadsheets and bank statements. I have texts and phone messages from her saying that she was going to ruin my life and make my life hell. My defense would be that Marlie O'Neal tried to frame me. I think a jury would believe that ..."

Beneath the table, Vivian twisted her wrists desperately, wildly, ignoring the burning pain.

"However, if you were called to testify against me," Stone said, "then that would be a problem. I Googled you. You're a very respected journalist. People trust you. Your entire career, before you came to this island, was devoted to uncovering corruption, collusion, and malfeasance. A jury would believe your testimony against me, which is why you can't be around to testify against me."

Stone turned and walked away from her, toward the garage door. Moments later, he opened the door, stepped into the garage, and closed the door behind him.

Vivian's heart pounded so loud she could hardly hear herself think. Several times, she brought her wrists to her mouth and used her teeth, hoping to tear through the fibrous tape.

Why had Stone left the kitchen? Why did he go out into the garage?

Vivian intensified her efforts to loosen the tape as another plan took root in her mind. She wasn't about to be slaughtered like some silent lamb. She was going to fight. As best as she could, considering her restraints, she was going to struggle and wrestle and scream bloody murder until she got the attention of every one of her neighbors.

The garage door opened and Stone walked back into the kitchen.

As she stared at the banker, the hopelessness she'd managed to keep at bay broke free, rushing toward her.

As he approached the table, Stone carried a large red plastic can in his left hand. In his right hand, Stone held a gun, the barrel pointed directly at her.

Chapter Forty-Seven

Terrified, Vivian asked, "So, what now, Dr. Stone? You're going to kill me? You're going to have the blood of three women and an officer of the law on your hands?"

"That deputy was in the wrong place at the wrong time," Stone said. "It was unfortunate, but ..."

With the gun still trained on her, Stone sidestepped across the kitchen and placed the red plastic can on the countertop near the sink.

Vivian's stomach twisted. "What is that?"

"Gasoline," he said, unscrewing the black top. "Highly flammable."

Recoiling from the thick, pungent smell, Vivian stared at him, horrified. "You're going ... to ... set me on fire? You're going to burn me alive?"

"I'm not that sick and twisted," he said. "I'm not going to burn you alive. That's a bit heinous, even for me. I'm going to be merciful and shoot you in the head first. Trust me, you'll be dead when the house goes up in flames."

"You don't have to kill me," Vivian said.

"You think I want to kill you? Well, I don't. It's just, what choice do I have? I'm not a monster, I'm practical. If I don't kill you, then you'll call the police, tell them everything you know, and then they'll arrest me. At my trial, you'll tell the jury that I killed Amal and Marlie and that fat cop who did a piss-ass job of protecting you."

"What if I promise not to testify against you," Vivian bargained. "You could leave St. Killian. I won't try to stop you."

"You think I'm that stupid?" He shook his head as he began a slow walk around the table, pouring gasoline for the ring of fire he planned to surround her with. "As soon as I'm gone, you'll find a way out of your restraints, and you'll call the cops."

"No, I won't," Vivian promised, desperate, coughing as the nauseating gas fumes wafted around her.

"Again, do you think I'm that stupid?" The banker stopped in front of her, gas can in one hand, the gun in another.

"Look, if you kill me, you might get away from the St. Killian police, but you didn't just steal from Amal. You took money from some other clients, too," Vivian said. "If Amal was able to find you, then eventually, one of those other clients might track you down once they realize that you stole from them, too. Don't kill me and I'll help you get away from them. I know places where you can hide, places where some crook would never think to look."

"But you'll know where I am," the banker said. "Which means you would have some leverage over me, to keep me in line, so ..." He shrugged. "Thanks but no ..."

The banker trailed off, frowning, his expression flickering from shock to consternation to rage as he stared at something behind her.

"How the hell did you get in here?" The banker asked.

Vivian gasped and looked back over her shoulder.

Hope, joy, and relief swelled within her.

Leo? Was he really here? But how? When? Trembling, Vivian stared at the man who would forever have her heart. Leo cut his gaze to her, and when their eyes met, Vivian knew she was safe now. Leo was here, and no matter what, everything would be okay. The love and concern and fierceness in his beautiful blue eyes gave her the courage to believe Leo would make sure nothing bad happened to her.

"Back door was open," Leo said, focused on Stone.

Stone rubbed his jaw, his shrewd gaze darting from Leo to Vivian and then back to Leo. His eyes were cool and appraising, but she saw frustration as he assessed the situation. Maybe he was having problems figuring Leo into his twisted, homicidal equation.

"Actually, it's good you're here."

"Is that right?" Leo asked, arms crossed over his chest.

"Saves me the trouble of having to hunt you down," the banker said. "I can just get rid of you right now."

"I'm not saving you any trouble," Leo said, glaring at Stone. "I'm bringing the trouble. The St. Killian police are right behind me, so you might as well—"

Stone splashed gasoline toward Leo. Vivian screamed, terrified by the gushing arc of flammable liquid, but Leo pivoted and the gas splattered against his shoulder and back.

Dropping the gas can, Stone grabbed Vivian and yanked her up from the table. He snaked an arm around Vivian's neck and pressed the barrel of the gun against the side of her head. Gasping from the cold steel near her temple, Vivian went rigid, staring at Leo, trying to draw courage and comfort from his presence, knowing he wouldn't let anything bad happen to her.

"Let her go ..." Leo warned.

"Not another step," the banker ordered, walking backward, dragging Vivian with him. "Don't make another move, or I'll put a bullet in her head."

"The hell you will," Leo said. "You kill her and then how will you get off this island? You need her alive, as a hostage, right?"

"I'll kill her after I get off the island," the banker said. "I'll send you a video."

"You want to get off this island," Leo said. "You let her go, and I'll drive you to the marina. My dad has a speed boat there. You can use it to go across to one of the other islands. St. Felipe might be your best bet. Customs officials there have been known to accept a bribe."

"Shut up!" The banker yelled, his hot, fetid breath slashing Vivian's cheek as he sidestepped toward the garage door. "Did I ask you for advice on how to get the hell off this island! I know how to disappear, okay? I don't need your help. All I need is—"

Faintly, in the distance, the wail of sirens interrupted Stone. Vivian felt his body tense, and she forced herself to stay still, praying his nerves wouldn't cause him to shoot her accidentally.

"Well, there's the trouble I promised," Leo said. "You're not getting away. You might as well—"

"I told you to shut the hell up!" the banker said, his breath expelling in short, ragged gasps as he walked backward, still dragging Vivian. "I am not going to jail. Not tonight, not ever. Now what I need you to do, if you don't want her brains splattered all over this room, is to go outside and tell those island pigs that I have a hostage and we need to negotiate or she dies."

The sirens howled louder as the police came closer. Moments later, red and blue lights shone through the living room window.

"Look, you want to take a hostage," Leo said. "Take me."

"What the hell are you talking about?"

"You need to take me," Leo said. "My mother is a billionaire. Aurora Nathaniel. I'm sure you've heard of her. She inherited Au'Naturale Cosmetics. You take me, and my mother will finance your escape to get me back."

Confused, Vivian stared at Leo. What the hell was he doing? Offering himself as a hostage?

"I don't believe you," the banker said, jumping as the police pounded on the door, demanding for him to come out with his hands up.

"I can get my mother on the line right now," Leo said, slowly making his way around the table. "Forget about negotiating with these island cops. They can't give you shit. My mother, on the other hand, can get you off this island, no problem. So, let Vivian go and take me."

"No, you can't," Vivian said. "Leo, what are you doing?"

"Grant Stone …" A disembodied voice, amplified by a bullhorn, penetrated the walls and seeped into the condo. "Come out with your hands up now! We have you surrounded!"

Stone cursed and then shoved Vivian away from him. Crying out, she stumbled and lost her balance, falling to the floor.

"Get your rich mother on the phone!" Stone ordered as he pointed the gun at Leo.

From her position on the floor, Vivian kicked her foot toward the banker's ankle, connecting with a hard kick to his shin. Caught off guard, Stone lurched forward, and Leo lunged at him, grabbing the barrel of the gun.

More pounding on the door mixed with the sounds of Leo and the banker grunting and wrestling for the gun.

"Grant Stone!" The police commands continued. "Come out with your hands up!"

After ramming his fist into the banker's stomach, Leo was able to grab the gun and slam it against the banker's head. Stone stumbled and threw a disoriented punch in Leo's direction, but Leo ducked and threw another punch of his own, which connected, smashing into Stone's jaw. The banker stumbled back into the refrigerator. Leo hit him again, leaving the banker dazed and tottering, until he dropped to his knees, panting, his right eye swollen and bruised, already starting to close.

Leo kicked the banker in the side. Stone toppled over and sprawled on the floor. Seconds later, the police barreled through the front door, guns drawn, barking commands and telling everyone to freeze.

Epilogue

Six Months Later

Lust flooded through Vivian's body, like a shot of adrenaline, leaving her dizzy and weak. She stared at Leo's ripped muscular chest and the defined six-pack contracting with each breath. His skin glistening, he looked like a personified Greek statue emerging from the crystal clear turquoise waters of the Caribbean Sea. Her attraction to him was too powerful and hypnotic.

She watched Leo, smiling as he approached her. Loosening the tie of his board shorts, he let them slide down his legs, stepping out of them as he continued his approach. His steps were slow and measured as the evidence of his attraction to her began to emerge slowly. Vivian felt her breath quicken at the sight of him, large and thick, her body responding in anticipation of the inevitable.

Vivian glanced around to ensure they were alone. The beach

was a hidden gem, known only to locals and completely deserted at this hour of the morning. The perfect backdrop for seduction.

As Leo reached the edge of the blanket, lowering his naked body against hers, she could feel him, hard and throbbing, and he placed his lips on hers with a feverish passion, seeking to devour all the love she was willing to give. His tongue was sending her into a frenzy as she trailed her tongue around the tip of his, sucking it gently, coaxing it in and out of her mouth.

Vivian barely had a moment to register the deft removal of her bikini, as she felt the cool breeze caressing her bare skin before he pressed his body against her once again. Seconds later, he rose up over her and entered her, kissing her as though his life depended on it. A moan escaped Vivian as she tried to meld her body with his.

Reciprocity of unconditional love between them heightened the ecstasy as they rode the wave of desire with reckless abandon. Vivian wrapped her legs around his waist as he continued to pleasure her, adjusting his pace to keep her on the edge, a careful balance of delicate abandon and fierce determination. Soon, they were both gasping and thrashing uncontrollably, as the sweet, blissful explosion of pleasure simultaneously detonated within them.

As Vivian's breathing returned to a normal pace, her eyes fluttered open. Struggling to focus, she blinked at the large round clouds moving quickly across the blue sky. Glancing away from the sun, her eyes settled on him.

Leo stared at her, a sly grin on his face. Leaning down he placed a soft kiss on her forehead and then trailed kisses in a zig-zag pattern across her face, gently covering her eyes, then her nose, and her cheeks before caressing her mouth.

Pulling back, Leo said, "I love you."

Vivian sighed. "I love you."

Collapsing down next to her, Leo pulled her into his arms and closed his eyes. After a few seconds, she could hear his rhythmic breathing as he drifted to sleep.

Smiling contentedly, Vivian wrapped her arms around Leo, burrowing her head into his neck. She couldn't believe how perfect her life was now. Six months ago, she hadn't even known if she would live to experience this blissful day in the arms of the man she would love forever.

The memories of that horrible night when Grant Stone had tried to kill her were finally starting to fade. Vivian had been able to overcome the trauma and focus on her relationship with Leo, resolving to let go of her fears and trust in their love.

After his arrest, Stone had been tried and convicted for the murders of Amal, Marlie O'Neal, and Deputy Hector Rambla. The homicidal banker was sentenced to life in prison, with no possibility of parole. Stone hadn't lasted long behind bars, though. Two months into his stint, he was killed during a riot in the prison recreation room.

Beanie had covered the story for the *Palmchat Gazette*. During his investigation, Beanie had found out, from a confidential source at the facility, that the riot had been a diversion so Stone could be murdered. Apparently, one of Stone's shady clients, a mobster based in Florida named Carmine D'Ambrosia, had ordered the hit after finding out about Stone's scheme to swindle him.

Leo yawned as he woke from his nap and then whispered. "I have news."

There was a strange look in his eyes, one Vivian couldn't quite read.

"What kind of news?" Vivian asked. No matter what Leo had to share, she knew they could overcome any challenges. They'd already been through so much, and their relationship was much stronger from it.

"I turned in my resignation to *The New York Times* ..." Leo said, hesitating as he looked at her. Vivian couldn't hide her shock and bewilderment from this unexpected act. Leo was walking away from the job he loved, and she knew there was only one reason. Clamping her hands against her mouth, Vivian allowed the tears to flow freely from her eyes as the depths of Leo's love for her were confirmed.

"I never want to be away from you," Leo said, brushing the tears away from her face. "St. Killian has a lot to offer, but more importantly, it's where you are. It's where we found our way back to each other, and it's where I'm going to be from now on."

"But what are you going to do here? Won't you be bored? I can't let you do this! I will move, you don't have to give up your career for me," Vivian pleaded, not wanting him to make such a huge, but unnecessary sacrifice.

"I'm not giving up my career. I'll be staying on as the editor-in-chief of the *Palmchat Gazette*," Leo said, as he ran his hands over her body, caressing her breasts with slow circles.

"You'll be my boss, permanently?" Vivian asked, raising an eyebrow.

"Only at work. You'll still call the shots at home, Mrs. Bronson." Leo winked at her.

"Seems like you have everything figured out, Mr. Bronson," Vivian said, as she pushed him over and straddled him. As she placed her hands on the sides of his face, the emerald cut diamond ring with matching diamond eternity wedding band on her left hand sparkled in the sun.

"Yes, I do," Leo said, pulled her down to him, and kissed her.

Note from Rachel & Angel

Thanks so much for taking the time to read Reunion Island. We hope you enjoyed it as much as we enjoyed writing it.

Honest reviews by readers are the most powerful way to help others discover our books. Please consider taking one minute to share your thoughts on the book by rating and reviewing it on Amazon.com.

We'd be eternally grateful!

Exclusive Offer from Rachel Woods

Rachel Woods has been entertaining readers with her brand of romantic suspense -- sexy dangerous fiction. Now you can get one of her books FLAWLESS MISTAKE for FREE, you just need to go to the link and tell her where to send it: http://eepurl.com/bxtIF9

And if you sign up for the mailing list, in addition to the FREE book, you'll also get all of this stuff:

- Access to Rachel's Flash Fiction for FREE, exclusive to her mailing list subscribers.
- Chance to win books and Amazon gift cards in Rachel's monthly giveaways.
- Invitation to join Rachel's advance readers team — Sexy Dangerous Partners.

What are you waiting for? Join today!

Also by Rachel Woods

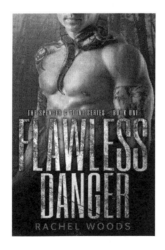

About the Author ~ Rachel Woods

Rachel Woods studied journalism and graduated from the University of Houston where she published articles in the Daily Cougar. She is a legal assistant by day and a freelance writer and blogger with a penchant for melodrama by night. Many of her stories take place on the islands, which she has visited around the world. Rachel resides in Houston, Texas with her three sock monkeys.

For more information:
www.therachelwoods.com
therachelwoodsauthor@gmail.com

About the Author ~ Angel Vane

Angel Vane has a dramatic personality, is prone to exaggeration and is in perpetual pursuit of her creative muse. She loves writing, reading, traveling, spa days and soap operas. Angel resides in Tomball, Texas.

For more information:
angelvaneauthor@gmail.com

About the Publisher

BonzaiMoon Books is a family-run, artisanal publishing company created in the summer of 2014. We publish works of fiction in various genres. Our passion and focus is working with authors who write the books you want to read, and giving those authors the opportunity to have more direct input in the publishing of their work.

To receive special offers, bonus content and news about our latest ebooks, sign up for our mailing list on our website.

For more information:
www.bonzaimoonbooks.com
bonzaimoon@gmail.com

Made in the USA
Middletown, DE
01 July 2018